# Death by Reunion

## A Jesse Clarke Mystery

### Helen Goltz

Atlas Productions

Death by Sugar

First published in 2021. Reprinted 2025.

Copyright © Helen Goltz



Cover art: Art by Karri – artbykarri.com

This book is a work of fiction. Names, characters, places and incidents are either the product of the author's imagination or are used fictitiously. Any resemblance to actual persons, living or dead, or to actual events or locales is entirely coincidental. Any medical experiments or results cited in this novel have been fictionalised and any slight of specific people, experiments, research or organisations is unintentional.

Dedicated to animal lovers everywhere

No animals, including Jesse's wonder dog Atlas, ever get harmed, dog-napped, threatened or die in these stories. Atlas lives on forever. So, rest assured, dear reader, and read on in peace.

I am a proud supporter of the WSPA (World Society for the Protection of Animals) and Animals Australia, and I thank them for their continued efforts to make the world kinder to animals.

# Chapter 1

THE TELEVISION STUDIO LIGHTS flashed for a few seconds, and people around me in the audience hushed. Melanie – my best friend – nudged me. She loved reality television, me… I could take it or leave it.

'So exciting,' she whispered. 'Definitely worth having the day off work to be here.'

'For sure,' I said. 'I love behind the scenes.' Which I did. Years of being in publicity gave me a backstage pass to lots of productions and events.

'I can't wait to watch it later on TV and see what made the cut,' Melanie added.

'Ready on set,' a man wearing headphones announced, and I leaned past Melanie to look to the left of the stage.

'Alex isn't here yet,' I whispered.

The *Lose it!* television production set was divided into three different areas – the *Lose it!* weight loss group had a stage with an enormous set of scales and a screen behind it that showed their weight; the *Lose it!* love group had a snug sitting room with red couches, and the *Lose it!* life group had a boardroom office setting.

All the teams seemed to be in place except the *Lose it!* weight loss group... or more specifically, Alex, my old school friend who was on the team working to get those kilos off.

'Hold up, we're missing one,' the floor manager yelled. I'm guessing it was the floor manager because he'd been bossing people around on the floor for the last twenty minutes.

'It's Alex, but he was finished in make-up; he should be here by now,' a large lady on the *Lose it!* team spoke up. She hadn't lost all her target weight yet, by the looks of it.

'I saw him upstairs,' someone else contributed, and the floor manager sighed loudly and dramatically. I expected him to say 'you pesky kids' next, but instead, he ordered one of the work experience girls to find Alex.

'Do you think he's dropped out?' Mel asked me.

'No way, he said he was determined to see it through.' I looked around the studio but didn't recognise anyone. I thought maybe some other school friends might have come. Alex managed to get a few extra tickets.

Then we heard it, a piercingly loud scream that sounded like something bad had happened. Something as bad as death.

# Chapter 2

ALEX BRYSON WAS DROP-DEAD gorgeous, literally – gorgeous and dead. The before-and-after photos of his weight loss were unbelievable, transforming his appearance completely. I pinned Alex's pictures on the whiteboard in my office with heart-shaped magnets – they were cheaper than the star-shaped ones – then I sat back on the edge of the desk and studied the photos and my handiwork. Nice work, me!

'Oh good, whiteboards, so we don't go off the rails,' Ed, my business partner, said as he entered the office. Ed didn't warm up until about 10am and he was even worse on a Monday, but we liked it was just the two of us, we didn't have to play nice if we didn't feel like it.

'Morning!' I said cheerily. It was part of my job as the business owner to motivate.

'Monday,' he responded and dropped into his chair, his satchel falling to the ground beside his desk. Despite the obvious stress of the beginning of the week, Ed looked trim, neat and pressed with his coloured-coordinated shirt and pants and every blonde hair in place. Damn him. Meanwhile, I'd tied back my straighter-than-straight brown hair into a ponytail, swiped on some makeup and declared the job done. It was hard to live up to Ed's standards, so I gave up some time ago and have had very few regrets.

'So, the new boards,' I said, waving a hand over them like a TV quiz show hostess. 'This board features our current publicity projects with our names assigned to them; the second board features my private investigator work.'

It was an odd business pairing, but I needed a change, so I took a private investigator course. Eighteen months later, I still love the mix of work.

'When did this happen?' Ed asked with a nod to my board.

'I was boyfriend-free for the weekend,' I said like that explained everything.

'Where was Dominic? You've finally scared him off, haven't you?'

I gave him a smirk. 'Dominic had a weekend boot camp,' I told Ed. 'He and some of the other personal trainers took fifty suckers – I mean clients – away for the weekend to exercise, eat properly, find themselves, you know that sort of thing.'

'Why didn't you go?' Ed asked and then laughed at the thought.

'I was very busy,' I told him. He pepped up when I reached for the coffee cup holder as if I were about to go do the coffee run. That was just a ruse to get his attention.

'I think I've remembered all our current projects,' I said, studying the right-hand side of the board. '*The Eat Local Week Festival* is yours; the Choir's *Mahler: Symphony No.2 – Resurrection* is mine, and Lord help me, I may need resurrection by the time I'm finished,' I said, and Ed chuckled. He loved that the choir's manager, Mona, always asked me to do the publicity so I couldn't palm it off on him. But I've had my revenge – a few months ago a guy who wrote a book on the history of fishing wanted it publicised and it was perfect for Ed. He did a very ef-fish-ent job!

I continued: 'The Water Boards' local *River Conservation Campaign* we do together; *Exotic Theatre*—' I gave Ed a look, and he grimaced.

'They are truly temperamental artists,' he grimaced, thinking about them. 'And to think I was so excited initially about taking them on. By the way, what's with the heart magnets?'

'Nothing, they were on sale,' I told him. 'They were six dollars cheaper than the star magnets! Why, I wonder?'

'Beats me. Love hurts,' Ed suggested.

'Yeah, that might be it.'

Ed rose and came over to my private investigator side of the board. He pointed to the photo of a guy who looked like he could audition for a *Superman* movie.

'So, who is that this hottie, and does Dom know you've got a half-naked, muscly guy heart-pinned to your whiteboard that is not him?' Ed studied the photo.

'It's business. I barely noticed he was half-naked or that he worked out.'

Ed scoffed.

'Fine then. This is Alex Bryson. I went to school with him, but trust me, he didn't look like that then. In fact,' I continued, 'if he had passed me on the street now, I wouldn't have recognised him!'

'But you would have looked.'

'If he had his shirt off. We must admire beauty; we'd do the same if a Mercedes Silver Ghost drove past,' I said, justifying myself.

'Indeed, we would.' Ed nodded, then added. 'I have no idea what a Mercedes ghost car looks like.' He waved his hand dismissively.

I pointed to Alex in the two school photos. 'And this is Alex as I remember him – a chubby kid and an overweight teenager.'

'Who's that geek?' Simon asked, looking over my shoulder at the class photo and pointing at a girl with hair pulled back severely and a very serious look on her face.

I gave him a wry look, and Ed laughed. He knew perfectly well who it was.

'That would be me. I was a very dedicated student.'

'How long since you've seen Alex?' Ed asked.

'Recently at our school reunion, but before that, not since school, a decade ago.' I sat back on the edge of my desk.

'Do you like him?' he asked soberly.

'He's the shy and quiet type. To be honest, I barely remember him from school. But he was the exact opposite at our reunion last month. He was quite popular, especially with the ladies.'

'I can see why,' Ed said. 'So, is Alex your new client? That beautiful specimen of manhood, I want to be in the office when he comes in.'

'No, Alex is dead.'

'No!' he gasped.

I nodded and felt a wave of emotions as I looked from his school photos to the photo of Alex now.

'How?' Ed asked. 'What happened?'

'A tragic accident, and exactly one week after our school reunion. But his parents don't believe it was an accident.'

'And that's where you step in?' he asked.

'I'm on the case.' I saw Ed's expression – a look that said I should get my priorities right. 'But I'm on the coffee run first.' That brightened him. Business as usual then.

# Chapter 3

ALEX HAD A MEDIA profile I was unaware of, but I confess that I don't watch much reality TV. He had his 15 minutes of fame – as Andy Warhol predicted we all had in the course of our lives – when the *Lose it!* TV producers accepted him on their reality program. I handed Ed his large coffee, which he inhaled like it was oxygen, before sipping it.

'So, what do we know about spunky Alex?' he asked as if we'd be working this case together, bless him.

I returned to my desk, lowered myself into my chair and turned to my new boards, which were still a novelty.

'Well, for starters, Alex went on the reality program, *Lose it!*'

'No!' Ed exclaimed.

'True story,' I said. 'Trust me, I am more surprised than you are. Alex was so quiet at school you'd barely know he was in the class, and then he goes on national television in a reality program!' I shook my head. 'People constantly surprise me, but usually for all the wrong reasons.'

'Ain't that the truth,' he agreed. 'So *Lose it!*, have you ever watched it?'

'Nope, have you?'

Ed looked embarrassed. 'I wish I could say no, but Simon loves reality television. He'll watch anything... dating shows, weight loss, cooking challenges, endurance and survival programs... God help me. Yes, even *Lose it!* But I don't remember Alex.'

'That's because the series he is in is still in production and hasn't hit our screens yet, but they have chosen the stars – if you can call them that,' I told Ed. 'They all have social media accounts created for them which show the *before* stuff, but because I saw Alex at our reunion, I've seen the *after* stuff.'

'Oh wow,' Ed said after a quick online hunt and finding Alex's page on *Lose it!* then glancing up at his photo on the board. 'He had to be in with a good chance to win it.'

'I'll have to watch past episodes; I've never seen it. Can you wrap it up in a nutshell?' I took a large sip of my skinny cappuccino, eagerly anticipating Ed's delivery.

'Sure,' Ed said, leaning forward and happy to accept the challenge. 'The concept is you come on the show, and you have to lose something – weight, a bad relationship or friendship, leave a job you hate and tell the boss why... whatever you nominate at the start, you have to do it in a three-month time frame and they track your journey plus all the emotional roll out from before and after.'

'Sounds horrendous, and all aired out in public!' I couldn't think of anything worse.

Ed agreed. 'I know, but it is addictive, and they edit out all the boring bits.'

'Right,' I said. 'Alex said there were two weeks left to go in production. I'm guessing he would have been in the weight loss challenge.'

'Correct,' Ed said like I was a game show contestant. '*Love* is relationship, family or friends. *Life* is the job scene, and *Loss* is body transformation, as they call it. There's a $50,000 prize for the winner of each category, and then there's the viewer's vote. The winner of that gets the top prize of $200,000.'

'Wow,' I said. 'Now I get why Alex signed up. If you are going to count calories and feel the burn, you might as well try for a cash cow at the same time.'

'Exactly. The program sucks you in. It's like you're taking the journey with them,' Ed said, 'but the weight loss ones are always the most fascinating because the before and after shots can be so dramatic. Alex's transformation is amazing.'

'Hmm,' I said, 'I wonder how competitive the fellow contestants are on that show.'

'Ooh, motive!' Ed said, getting swept up in our discussion. He looked at Alex's photo again and sighed. 'So, how did he die?'

'He tripped down the stairs at the television studio,' I said. 'He had supposedly just left the makeup room and was heading to the studio to go on live.'

'Get out of here,' Ed said.

'True story. But the manner of his death is all very hush-hush. The producers are cutting him out of the footage and substituting another contest. It's a huge job, apparently.'

'That's one hell of a stage exit.' Ed frowned at the thought.

'Especially when he was fit,' I agreed. 'You'd think he'd be a little more agile.' We stared at Alex's photo for a moment, and then I sighed. 'I'll have to read everything I can get my hands on now about Alex before I meet with his parents on my way home this afternoon.'

'I'll send you the link for the TV show,' Ed said, and I thanked him.

It is anyone's guess how Alex's parents came across me, except that I went to school with their son. I wasn't sure what they wanted me to do when the police had closed the case and declared it an accident. I'm guessing that they thought there was more to his death and wanted to hire me – I know, I'm all over this private detective thinking. But if they had nothing to reveal except their grief, I suspect the case might be closed before it was opened.

~ ele ~

I arrived at Alex's parents' apartment at 4.30pm for my appointment. His parents looked like the walking grief-stricken – exhausted, thin, and strangely alike. They say good couples looked alike, or did they eventually look like their pets? Hmm, it's a good thing then that Dominic and Atlas are both good-looking.

Jenny Bryson placed mugs of tea in front of me and her husband, Gary, then returned to the kitchen for her own and a plate of biscuits before sitting back next to me. I thanked her and declined the offer of a biscuit. I really wanted one, but it always seemed inappropriate to eat a jam drop or nut swirl biscuit when someone was talking about a tragedy.

Part of the living room was a shrine to their son, Alex; the rest was bland. I sat back and took in the room; there wasn't much to take in – it was like a modern art gallery – all white, with mirrors and glass, and several large artworks on display. I expected a tour group to come through at any moment, following the person in front holding an umbrella. Where was I? Right, I kicked off our meeting.

'Thank you for trusting me with your concerns, but can I ask why you need me when the police have already investigated Alex's death?'

Jenny gave Gary a nod, and he cleared his throat and explained.

'Alex's death initially looked like an accident. We couldn't believe he had an enemy in the world, and he was passionate about his newfound fitness. He was careful. He ran steps regularly as part of his workout, including those steep ones at the cliff – he did those with gym mates several nights a week. I don't understand how he could just topple down the studio stairs, and that's it... his life gone like that,' he said and clicked his fingers, his voice ending on a high and angry note.

Jenny continued. 'Our son was very comfortable in his new fit body and wouldn't do anything to harm himself. He was really loving his life and his work.'

'Alex was a pilot, wasn't he?' I asked.

'Yes,' Jenny said, looking as proud as punch. 'Mostly domestic routes these days, which he preferred because he liked to catch up with friends, go to the gym, all the usual stuff you should do at his and your age. This TV show was taking up way too much of his time, but there were only a few weeks left, and Alex was doing so well.'

'And the police report,' I said, bringing them back to the cause of death. 'They found nothing suspicious?'

Gary shook his head. 'No. There were lots of people going up and down the stairs, given that the green room, the studio floor, and the makeup room were all accessible by that same flight of stairs. They were those metal type of stairs, with an iron handrail on both sides. A few witnesses said he'd been chatting to other contestants just before he fell, but mind you no one else fell. He had bruises all over him, so they couldn't conclusively say if he had been pushed.'

*My memories were different. All the contestants were in the studio except for Alex. Still, I'm unsure what Gary and Jenny hoped I could do.* Gary read my thoughts.

'We are not saying this is going to be easy and maybe the police are right, it was an accident – Alex lost his footing, but we want to exhaust that avenue. We want to bury our son knowing exactly what happened or if it was more sinister, we want that person outed, and we want someone punished.'

Gary was a big man in his mid-fifties but looked mid-sixties, overweight like his son once was and with thinning strands of hair.

'I'll be upfront,' he continued and glanced at Jenny, who frowned. 'I think you are too young for this job – I'd rather be a seasoned detective. But given you knew Alex and some of his school friends, we figured you might have an insider chance of getting information.'

I nodded, glad we got that out in the open. I'd worked with men like Gary before who were in positions of power and liked to remind you of that. For a few moments, bossy Gary and I talked about terms, price, and access to reports, and we settled on all aspects. I carried on.

'Did Alex have a partner?' I asked.

'Several,' his mother said. 'No one he had brought home yet for us to meet, but some he had mentioned in passing. He said they were just work friends. There was a flight attendant named Tara, a girl he worked out with, and Casey or Cassie? But no, as for love interests, nothing serious yet.' And then she realised that the 'yet' would never eventuate – no wedding or grandchildren were coming, and she became more emotional.

'I'm so sorry,' I said, reaching for her hand.

'I'm sure Lucy was trying to keep him in her clutches,' Gary said.

'Lucy?' I asked with interest.

'His estranged wife,' Gary said.

*Wife! What the hell? That might have been handy if his parents had mentioned earlier in the discussion that he was married or separated.*

Jenny's lips thinned. 'Lucy, yes, they separated about the time Alex took an interest in his fitness. They were never suited; she was always so loud and had to be the life of the party. Alex was more conservative and dignified.'

'So, you don't think that Lucy had any part in Alex's death?' I asked.

Gary scoffed. 'Other than nagging him, embarrassing him by showing up at his work and demanding to know if he was having an affair, and in general being a pain in his side, no, I think she is in the clear.'

'She knew he was applying for the *Lose it!* program?' I asked, feeling sad for Lucy. She had the rug pulled from under her by the sounds of it.

'She sure did,' Gary answered. 'It caused a lot of problems. I guess she saw the writing was on the wall.'

I must have looked blank because Gary elaborated. 'The management warned Alex that he had to lose some weight or he wouldn't be allowed to fly. Technically, on commercial flights, there's no pilot weight limit, but they were talking about wellness and all this crap. I told Alex they probably couldn't make it stick, but he wanted to do something about his weight.'

Jenny continued. 'One of the other pilots suggested he should enter *Lose it!* We were fully supportive of it, excited really, thinking that he might get financially ahead, feel better about himself and be open to a new love.'

Gary agreed. 'Alex invited Lucy to train with him, but she didn't want to, so you can imagine how that played out.'

'I'd like to contact her nevertheless,' I said, and Jenny rose, got her details, scribbled them on a piece of paper, and handed them to me.

'Don't waste too much time on her; we're paying you to get a result, and she's a dead-end,' he snapped, and Jenny looked embarrassed.

'I need to talk to her. You don't know what she might be privy to or have witnessed,' I told Gary.

He made a grunting sound as if he'd indulge me. It was no big deal; I'm used to horror clients – some of them think they owe you when they hire you. Luckily, Ed and I were in a wonderful position now, and we no longer have to work with them. Life was too short.

'Did you retrieve any of Alex's emails and phone messages?' I asked, and Jenny answered.

'The police have them, but since they declared it an accident, you can request them back.' Jenny took a deep breath. 'I believe you can help us, Jesse, I really do.' Ah, God, raw grief was awful.

'I'll do anything to help and honour Alex's memory.'

'Thank you,' she said after blowing her nose.

I left them with a list of things I needed, including the names of people in Alex's life, the places he went, the gym where he trained, his online password if they knew it and a few other things. I stopped at the door on my way out and said: 'Can I ask how you heard about me?'

Jenny smiled. 'My sister-in-law is the best friend of one of your previous clients, and when we heard you went to school with Alex, it was perfect.'

'Oh, well, that's great. Word of mouth,' I said. I had no idea who she was talking about, but I'd work that connection out later. As I left them with a little more hope in their eyes, I realised I would have to get back in touch with all my old school friends who went to the reunion to ask if they had talked with Alex on the night. And I thought seeing everyone again just that one night was bad enough.

'I love school reunions,' Dominic said.

'Don't be ridiculous, no one loves school reunions,' I said, looking at him like he was an alien – a tall, good looking, dark-haired, blue-eyed alien from planet Spunky.

We were out walking Atlas, the wonder dog, at the end of our day. Dom rarely came along on our walk because he was working, but he got an early mark after running nutrition lectures at schools instead of running classes. So tonight, Atlas and I had to talk about subjects that could involve him. I nearly fell over Atlas as he stopped to sniff a pole. Dom caught me, settled a kiss on the top of my head, and carried on.

'What's not to like about a reunion?' he continued. 'It's great catching up with everyone again after all the years and seeing what they are all doing with their lives.'

'What a charming childhood you must have had,' I said and patted his nice tight butt because I could legally since we were a couple. 'I bet you were everyone's friend and got on with the guys and girls; I bet you always looked this gorgeous. No glasses, pimples or awkward growth spurts, and you got picked for teams every time.'

He smiled, thought about what I said for a few minutes, and then answered: 'Yeah.'

'Shut up,' I told him, and he laughed.

'Come on, you can't tell me you had it that hard. Bet you were a cute little thing and smart too.'

'I had a boy's name, for starters. I'm no princess, but I don't like balls being thrown at me, so contact sports were out. Paul Murphy told everyone I kissed him and had bad breath, so I always had sore gums from brushing. That's just skimming the top. But poor Alex...'

'What was Alex's story?'

'He was an overweight kid from grade one and would always get picked on. He wasn't fit enough to participate in sports, he was smart, which was not cool when you are overweight and nerdy, and he was shy. I remember little more about him, to be honest.'

'It's a familiar story,' Dom said. 'I see it every day at the gym in some form or another.'

We were coming to the turnaround point of our walk, and I let Atlas lead the way; he knew the route like the back of his paw.

Dom continued. 'I'm guessing that the coroner and doctor looked for genetic conditions, something that might make Alex collapse and fall down the stairs?'

'I don't know. I'm yet to see the report. But he's an only child; I think his weight was from over-pampering, not a genetic issue. Still, his folks are convinced it's not an accident.'

'Can't blame there. What next then?' he asked. I loved that Dom always got involved in my work; he felt the need to be my bodyguard.

I shrugged and teasing him said: 'I'll have to go to the TV studio, plus his gym, and question guys with muscles – horrendous.'

Our small cottage came into view, dwarfed by two-storey houses on either side. A lamp's light shone through the front window, and the small porch and stairs invited us into the warmth inside. I loved our home. Atlas slowed down and sniffed everything in sight. It's his ploy as we get closer to home so he can stay out longer... I'm on to him.

Dom cleared his throat. 'I could... you know... show you some of those muscles first hand if that helped with your research?' he offered with a grin.

'Oh my, that would be a big help,' I brightened.

'Anything to help,' Dom said, and we hurried. Research, after all, was a really important part of my job.

# Chapter 4

I STOPPED DEAD. A woman a head taller than me, about twice as wide, and with a buzz haircut blocked the doorway. She stood, arms crossed in front of her chest, highlighting the tattoos running up her forearms.

'Intruder!' she said in a low, menacing voice. I looked around. Yep, she was definitely talking to me.

'Ah, no, Veronica, the producer, signed me in,' I said, waving the folder in my hands like that proved it.

Ed rolled his eyes. 'An intruder is a wildcard entry. Two people score wildcards during filming, and they join the show after it's started, shake it up and have a chance to win the prizes.'

I looked at Ed. 'Well, that hardly seems fair.'

'Exactly,' the tattoo girl agreed.

'It's for the TV ratings,' Ed said.

'Oh.' I turned back to the tattoo girl. 'I'm not in the TV show; I'm Alex's friend.'

'Bit late then, he's dead,' she said and stepped back to let us pass.

'So, you've opted to *lose* your tact for the show, have you? You're a winner for sure!' I snapped, and I heard Ed's breath hitch. He often reminded me he was not Dominic and could not save me in a fight.

She glared at me and then grinned. 'You've got spunk, I like you.' With that, she turned and left. Ed and I breathed again. He gave me a pained look.

'What? Imagine if I didn't know Alex was dead. That's a bad way to find out.' I nudged him along and we entered and found a seat in the studio in almost the same location I sat with Mel.

'It's weird how pokey it all looks when you are behind the scenes,' Ed said.

'I know. It takes all the glamour out of it,' I agreed.

I was here on official business this time, trying to determine if any of Alex's fellow competitors wanted to win badly enough to get him knocked out of the competition. I knew for a fact, because I was in the studio the day Alex died, that none of them were with him at the time... but that doesn't mean they didn't conspire to get rid of him. Ed had insisted on coming so he could tell Simon all about it. We isolated ourselves from the dozen other family and friends sitting in the studio seats to check everyone out without being caught in the act. I opened the folder and pulled out the list of contestants that the producer, Veronica, gave me. She had been an amazing help – I suspect she wanted to keep it all under tabs.

'Goody, she's put pics in,' I said, showing Ed. I found my new friend, tattoo girl. She wasn't in Alex's group; she was in the *Love* group.

'I wondered if she is gaining or losing a lover or friend,' I mused.

Ed shuddered at the thought. 'So, who am I looking out for?' he asked, narrowing his eyes and looking more like a suspicious spy than a publicist.

'There are only three genuine threats to the prize, according to Veronica, so that makes it easier,' I told him. 'The two vying for the top position in Alex's weight loss category are Whitney and Ryan.' I showed Ed their photos. Lowering my voice, I read the summary included of the potential assassins: 'Whitney is a single mum of three trying to get her life and health back on track and has lost the most weight to date, even more than Alex, so she's in the lead to win the $50,000 in her category.'

Ed nodded. 'Her motive for murder is the desire to stay in top place, and she's got three kids to feed.' We both looked at Whitney, who was talking with some of the other contestants on stage. She was a big woman with brown skin, hair tied back tightly, and a big laugh. She came across as warm and popular.

'Can't see it,' I whispered.

'Nuh, me either. Next.'

'Ryan Anderson,' I said, and we both looked at his photo and then looked up at him on stage. Ryan was in his mid-forties, balding, and still pretty big. He stood with his arms folded, looking impatient like he had ten better places to be. Whitney tried to engage him in the group's conversation, and he gave her one of those chin-up movements and a brief smile, then went back to looking disinterested.

Ed opened his phone and went to the social media page. He pointed at a photo of Ryan. 'It looks like he's lost a fair bit, but he still has a bit to lose.'

I agreed. 'I suspect he wouldn't be in the running for the top prize if Alex weren't out of the picture.'

We both looked at each other and gave a brief nod. He was a suspect. We'd be sure to talk with them both, but Ryan looked like someone who meant business.

'The only other person who has a real chance to take out the overall popularity prize of $200,000 because she's already got so many followers is in a different group – the love group,' I told Ed. 'Mimi Martinez – she's ditching her husband, who has had a few affairs and wants to find herself.' I looked up and checked out Mimi. Small, thin, mousey, barely noticeable Mimi.

Ed frowned. 'She looks like she's had the world on her shoulders. I think she'd be happy to break free money or no money. Can't see her bumping off Alex, too nervy,' he said.

'No, me either, but she might have had a gutful of guys and thought Alex was another one with attitude and wanted him out of her way.' I shrugged. Neither of us was convinced.

We stopped talking as they started recording, and after filming the first segment, I caught Veronica's eye. She waved us both down behind the stands.

'I can take you to the green room if you want to talk with any of them during the break. Of course, they can refuse to talk with you,' she said.

'Sure, I can find my way there; you're busy,' I said. She looked slightly worried at the idea and then glanced up the stairs.

They don't like to let you wander the corridors in television, you might wander on to a set and find yourself reading the news!

'Actually, that would be helpful,' she said. 'Straight up there.'

I nodded. 'We're on our way. We'll only be ten minutes or so and see ourselves out.'

'Great, let me know if you discover anything. I've got to let the marketing crisis management team know, and the psychologist and solicitor, yaddah, yaddah,' she waved her hand and departed. Ed and I headed upstairs.

✳

I thought Ryan might be our toughest customer, but not so. He looked me up and down and became Mr Charming.

'I liked Alex,' he said. 'Nice enough guy, but I'll be honest with you, the money would be great but I do alright in that regard. Got myself a building company and a few staff working for me.'

'Good on you,' I said like a fan girl since I suspected he was keen to impress. 'What made you join the show, then?'

'I got into bad habits, working late, eating crap, drinking a lot,' he leaned forward and lowered his voice. 'The standard of chick I was attracting was nothing to look twice at, so now, things are changing. You wouldn't believe the girls approaching me, and the show hasn't aired yet.'

Ed gave him a half-smile and encouraging nod that said 'you go for it' but knowing Ed, it meant, 'you're an idiot.'

Ryan needed very little encouragement to talk about himself, and then he asked if I was single. Blessedly, no.

'Want to know something?' he asked, 'in complete confidence?'

'Sure,' I said, leaning in closer, relieved at last that he might give me some insight into Alex's death.

'As soon as this is over, I don't give a crap how much I've learned about healthy eating. I'm going out for the biggest burger I can find. I could eat a cow.'

I pulled away and grinned. 'Good luck with that,' I said.

Bummer, so much for a clue. But in a way, he gave me one. He didn't mention money. He didn't say, 'After this is over and I've won the cash'… for Ryan, it appeared to be all about the girls… and cows. We thanked him and left Ryan to respond to his girl fans on his phone.

Whitney gave us both a kiss on the cheek. Whitney was so lovely that I refused to believe she could be involved.

She sighed, remembering Alex. 'He was a sweet and sensitive guy; we clicked from the start,' she said and smiled. Whitney leaned in to share a secret. 'I often attract the quiet ones because they just have to stand beside me, laugh, nod and say nothing, and I make enough noise for all of us.'

We laughed along because she was lovely. Did I mention that?

'I know you didn't know Alex that well, but did you see anything strange? Was anyone hanging around him you thought looked shifty or made him uneasy?' I asked.

Whitney shook her head. 'Sorry, darling, no. He had some gym friends in here, a girl who could have been his friend, sister or wife – I don't know, and his parents came along a couple of times, but they all seemed to get on.'

I nodded. 'How are you coping with it all?' I was just curious; I didn't expect her answer to break the case wide open.

She leant in closer. 'Have you ever dieted, darlin'?'

I nodded. 'Done a few of them,' I said. 'All I could think about was food.'

'Exactly!' she said, clapping her hands like I was a genius. At last, someone recognised that. Whitney continued: 'Well, you'll understand what it is like. Only amplify that by a thousand because you've got a big spotlight on you,' she said. 'Jesse, I am starving, but the thrill of fitting smaller clothing sizes keeps me going. I'm going bikini shopping as soon as this show wraps up. I don't care if I'm too old or curvy, I feel great!'

'Good on you,' I grinned, caught up in her enthusiasm. I thought of my boring swimming rashie at home. But sun protection was important!

I loved Whitney, and she would not likely be Alex's killer if I took her at face value. Ed gave me a discreet look that concurred with my sentiments. Last was Mimi – a nervy little woman focussed on the big picture.

'It's life-changing for us all,' Mimi told us. 'It is a privilege that we got picked to go on the show. The money would be great, I'd love to win it, but I'd like Whitney to win it too, she's got three kids.'

Hello, Saint Mimi! She was clearly a gentle soul and probably had been taken advantage of her whole life. But still, I had to be thorough.

'But you have children too,' I added, prodding to get an insight into delicate Mimi.

'Mine are all teens or older and making their own way in the world. Besides, I will get some alimony when I'm officially divorced. Whitney's a single mum, and that's a tough gig, so I'd rather she won than any of the others. No offence, I know Alex was your friend.'

'That's all good,' I told her, asking the same question about Alex's moods, guests, and what she might have observed.

'He brought friends to the recordings but only had his parents here on the weigh-in days. He was embarrassed, I think. To be honest, I barely knew him. We were in different *Lose it!* groups, and the groups don't mix much.'

I thanked her, and Ed and I saw ourselves out.

'What do you think?' Ed asked me when we got back to the car.

'I think I can lose *Lose it!* from my queries for now. Worst luck,' I sighed. 'I was hoping something obvious would leap out and grab me, but nope, I'm drowning in a sea of nothing.' I turned to him. 'Have you ever dieted?'

'No, Simon and I don't say the D-word. Simon prefers to call it a health kick,' Ed rolled his eyes, and I laughed. 'My kind of diet is a liquid diet.'

'Really?' I asked, surprised.

'Yes, after four drinks, I don't care how much I've eaten!'

—ee—

While sitting with Dominic on our couch, eating our chicken stir-fry that night, I contemplated the day.

'What are you thinking about,' Dom asked me. I must have looked intense or was staring off into space.

'Isn't that a chick question? What are you thinking about?'

'I was wondering what you were thinking,' he answered.

'Oh, well, that's boring. I was thinking about all the extras on set today... you know the consultant roles on *Lose it!* – trainers, dieticians, psychologists – they do pretty well out of those programs, don't they?'

'Hell yeah,' he answered, 'they are on camera, getting seen, building their profiles, releasing products in their name, doing appearances, all that sort of thing. And they get paid for being there as well.' He paused between mouthfuls of chicken and vegetables and added: 'It's not something I'd want to do, but if you were ambitious and loved the limelight, I can see why it would appeal. Was Alex like that or becoming like that?'

'I don't know, I doubt it. Why doesn't a TV role interest you? You're gorgeous; they would lap you up.' He gave me a grin.

'You're not biased at all, but thanks.' Dominic shrugged. 'I guess for the same reason I don't want to stay in this line of business in the long term – it's nice to turn people's lives around and get them fit, but it's exhausting when you have to motivate them all the time. You know, when they are lazy or whinging about having to do the exercises. Why bother coming unless you give it your all? You may as well have stayed home sitting on your couch with your takeaway.'

'Hmm,' I said, 'spoken like someone who has never had to watch his weight or refuse a doughnut in his life!' I prodded his lean body.

Dom chuckled. He finished his stir-fry and put the bowl on the coffee table. 'So, if I was a consultant on the program, what could I help you lose?'

'Ooh, tough question,' I said. I thought about it for a few moments while I finished dinner, and then, putting my empty bowl down, I shook my head. 'Nah, nothing. I'm happy in love, at home and work. I even like my friends.'

'I can think of something,' Dom said.

'Really?' I asked, surprised. 'What?'

He grabbed me and pulled me closer. 'Lose the clothes!'

I laughed but stopped him.

'We can't do that right now after eating. We have to wait at least thirty minutes before exercising, or is that just before swimming?'

'That's an old wives' tale,' Dom assured me, but I stayed resolute.

'I'm not risking it,' I teased him. 'I don't want to get a performance cramp. But if you wanted to do the dishes, that might be enough time to wait...'

His eyes narrowed, and he gave me a suspicious look.

I think I won that round.

# Chapter 5

I ALWAYS FELT OVERWHELMED with a fresh case, and now was no different. I heard the lift doors open at the end of the hallway; Ed might be back from his meeting. My ears were finely attuned to the sound, especially if I was in the office alone. It was a timing thing – it took arrivals about five seconds to reach the architect's office, about eight seconds to the accountant's door, and if I didn't hear those doors open or knocking, I knew they were coming to me, and it didn't sound like Ed's footfall. A large rap on my office door answered that question; I rose and called out, 'Come in' at the same time.

The door opened with a rush, and a lady in a black pantsuit with ginger hair, a ruddy complexion and a loud voice barged in!

Angela Cunningham.

All my memories of Angela from high school were of her barging... she was a born leader and liked to take charge.

'Jesse, I'm glad I caught you,' she said. 'I was going to call, but I was coming this way and thought I would just take a gamble you were in.'

'Angela, hi, it paid off. Will you have tea, coffee, juice or water?' I said, running through our standard top-shelf offers.

'Water would be a godsend, thank you.'

'Take a seat,' I said, indicating our small meeting table. I heard her sit with a sigh as I got us both a glass of cold water. Angela was the school captain in my final year and the organiser of our recent ten-year high school reunion. She was a teacher now, which wasn't surprising because she needed a job where she could organise people, and students had to obey most of the time.

'You're on school holidays?' I asked, returning, putting the water down in front of Angela and sitting opposite.

'Thank you,' she said, swallowing half the glass in three big sips. 'Yes, but it's just the students having a holiday. I've got so much class prep to do, and I'm on my way to look at some new teaching resources that have just come in at the head office. But I wanted to talk with you about Alex.'

'Great,' I said, now interested. I'm so desperate I'll talk to anyone. I'm fairly sure I didn't say that out loud. 'Thanks again for doing such a great job with the reunion. It was so much work, I imagine.'

'Oh, not really, but thanks. I had help, and I enjoyed doing it,' she said and continued: 'I dropped in to check on Alex's parents and offer my condolences, and they said you were on the case. I didn't know there was a case. I heard he fell, and the injury was fatal.'

'That might be all there is to it, but they're grieving,' I said, trying to quell any rumours or hope that might imply that I had found something incriminating. 'But I'm really glad you came by, Angela because I was going to call you for a list of everyone who came to our reunion and their contact details so I could ask them if they spoke with Alex that night and their impression of his state of mind, you know, that sort of thing,' I said waving my hand like that was what everyone did when they were investigating.

'I guessed as much,' she said, reaching down near her feet and picking up a large taupe tote bag. She pulled out some paperwork. 'This is a copy of the attendees and their contact details, including mobile numbers and emails,' she handed over five or six pages of paper.

'Angela, you're brilliant, thank you.' I happily took the material from her. 'I also wanted to ask if you saw anything suspicious, like maybe tension arising between Alex and anyone else?'

She took another mouthful of water and sat back before answering. 'No, but he was so different, wasn't he?'

'So different,' I agreed, 'as though his new appearance gave him the confidence to be more outgoing.'

'Yes,' she agreed, 'to be someone completely different. I see it all the time with my students. Sometimes, they are painfully shy or awkward, and then they'll get a role in the school play where they can step out of being themselves into another character, and you barely recognise them. It reminded me of Alex.'

'Yes,' I agreed, 'that's a good analogy – as if he was taking on a new role.'

'What I thought was odd was that Alex talked to Trent and Trad at the reunion. I had to look twice,' Angela said.

I groaned. It was an involuntary thing every time I thought about the two school jocks and their big egos.

'Was it friendly talking?' I asked.

Angela pursed her lips to think and answered: 'Well, I didn't notice it was heated, so it must have just been a normal conversation.'

'Still, that's interesting,' I said. 'Those guys wouldn't have noticed Alex at school, but now they all had their fitness in common.' I wondered if Trent or Trad suggested working out together.

'Oh, they noticed him at school,' Angela said in a less than impressed voice. 'They threw poor Alex into the girls' toilets a lot, as I remember.'

'Now that you mention it,' I said, agreeing, 'Alex and his friends were regular visitors there. By chance, are there any reunion photos I could access besides what we all snapped on the night?'

'Yes, there's a stack of photos up on the Facebook school reunion page.'

I cringed, having to look at them, everyone trying so hard to look fabulous, including me.

'We also had an event organiser for our reunion, she'll have some photos and footage, it is worth a try,' Angela said as if she knew all the desperate avenues I would travel down. I pictured myself in a car out of control heading to avenues with signage saying *'Desperate Street'*, *'No exit'* and *'One way only'*.

Then, what Angela said struck me. 'We had an event organiser?' I asked, surprised.

'Yes. *Party People*. You know the $70 we all paid to go along that night?' She didn't wait for an answer. 'Well, $40 went to an event organiser and the other $30 to drinks and nibblies. The event organiser found the venue, caterer, and DJ, got permission for a party, hired staff to serve, and organised decorations and cleaners. A godsend.'

She pulled a card from the oversized tote bag and gave it to me. 'Their contact details.'

'You're fantastic, thank you,' I said, glancing down at the card, which read: *Gabi Gordon, Owner and Chief Party Person, Party People.*

'My pleasure. It might lead to nothing, but every bit helps. That's what I tell my parent committees all the time about volunteering and monetary donations.' Angela sighed and rose, grabbed her bag and headed to the door. 'Well, must go,' she said.

I got up and followed, holding the contact list and card.

'Thank you, Angela; I really appreciate these and that you took the time to drop by.'

'Happy to help, Jesse. I hope you can find something to tell Alex's parents. Good luck with Gabi from *Party People* – she's one of those exhausting influencer types,' she said with a flap of her hand as if it was all too much. I smiled. I knew them well, and Angela was too pragmatic for that walk of life. The lift arrived in seconds, and with a wave, she had gone as quickly as she came.

Right, I needed to get my party on and see the *Party People.*

# Chapter 6

My best friend Melanie's name came up on my screen as I was driving to meet the Chief Party Person; I accepted the call.

'Hi, Mel!' I answered, but Mel rarely said hello. She just talked like we'd been interrupted last time and she picked up from there.

'I just finished a tax project that I started last week and I cannot see straight for numbers swimming before my eyes. I think I've become a human calculator, I had to tell someone, I'm losing my humanity—'

'—Is that you, Mel?' I cut her off and she thanked me.

'Phew, I was getting hysterical then. I need a coffee or the weekend, or both. Where are you by the way?'

Mel often had several trains of thought going at once, and many never reached their destination station.

'I am off to see the Chief Party Person of *Party People*,' I said, talking too loudly because I felt the need to shout when driving hands-free. The voice remote was at least a ruler's length from my mouth – ruler. Ha, the reunion had put me straight back in class mode.

'Ooh, I'd love that on my business card – Chief Party Person,' Mel said.

'I know, so cool. I've arrived, I'll tell you more later.'

'Party on,' she said and disconnected.

I drove up the driveway arched with trees and found a delightful little red house converted to a business at the end of the drive. I parked in one of the three spots marked for visitors and headed in. The front was all glass and there were three girls and a young guy all inside, beavering away on their laptops. Party people working for the Chief Party Person I imagine.

They weren't expecting me; I found in the spy business it was best not to make appointments so people don't prepare. Chief Party Person Gabi was 'out the back' taking photos for their social media account, posing with some new party props and sets that had arrived. Her staff member took me down the back path where there were party samples like marquees, bird baths, stages, and mirrors, and then a very glamorous woman gave me an exaggerated wave and held up her finger for one more minute. A young guy snapped away on his phone while she posed.

'I'll leave you here then,' the young minion who escorted me said, and I thanked her.

I could see what Angela, my former school captain, meant. She and Gabi could not be less alike. Gabi was slim, mid-thirties, had a body to die for, blonde shoulder-length hair cut to a dramatic edge and was made up to within an inch of her life. She was almost with me when she stopped to get a selfie next to one of those trees that were pruned to a perfect circle... the name will come to me... yep, arborists, your job was safe.

'That'll be plenty, Sax, thank you,' Gabi said, and Sax and his phone departed with a smile my way.

'Hi Gabi, I'm Jesse Clarke—'

'Jesse, don't tell me, let me guess,' she said and looked at my naked hand. 'An engagement party! Ooh, great timing, we just did the most romantic and amazing engagement party ever with an over-the-moon theme,' she sighed.

'Ah no, actually—'

'Wedding!' she clapped her hands together. 'Even better. We can do dignified, fun, escapist, glamorous, or all of those combined,' she said and gave a bubbly laugh.

'No, not a wedding, I was hoping—'

She cut me off again. I hoped to get a word in, but she looped her arm through mine and started touring me around their garden.

'Well, my last guess and then I'll give in – a milestone birthday! I'm guessing you are too young for a 30th, and you are not 18 or 21?'

'Reunion,' I said, 'My school reunion. Angela Cunningham said to—'

She dropped my arm and gasped. 'Darling, you've missed it; it was a few weeks back.'

'I was there; it was great. You did a brilliant job. Thank you,' I assured her, and she exhaled, put her hand on her heart, and smiled, pleased with my praise.

'I'm sorry to come unannounced, but I was hoping to see any photos or footage you might have, uncut ideally.'

'Oh, why didn't you say so! Absolutely. We have a viewing room where our clients can watch the footage – a lot of brides and grooms like to, but then they realise after watching about thirty minutes of the relatives dancing that they'd prefer to see our final cut package.'

Gabi started walking back to the viewing room and invited me to follow.

'Was there anything in particular you were looking for?' Before I could answer she called out: 'Sax can you load Angela Cunningham's uncut reunion footage to monitor one?'

"Overworked Sax" got up and headed to the viewing room, and we followed. I told her about Alex, and she went through all the emotions of shock, sadness, and curiosity and then offered any help she could.

'So, do you investigate all sorts of matters – big, small, different?' she asked, narrowing her eyes as she studied me.

'Absolutely nothing is off-limits,' I said, thinking of Dom rolling his eyes and shaking his head at that comment.

'I might have something I want to talk with you about... an incident that happened recently at a reunion, *my* family reunion. Got a business card?' she asked.

'Sure,' I said, grabbing one from the wallet in my carrying folder. She tucked it straight into her pocket without looking at it and thanked me.

'I have back-to-back meetings this afternoon, but just let my staff know when you are finished. I'll be in touch, but don't forget,' Gabi said, and tapped my hand, 'if you would like to talk with us about an engagement party...'

'Absolutely, you're my first port of call,' I agreed enthusiastically, smiling like it would happen next week. I thought of Dom's enthusiastic reaction to that idea, too. I made a note to send Gabi my rates in case she wanted to hire me for her family reunion problem... Lord knows what investigation that required... did someone steal Grandma's family recipe? That would make for a pleasant change; Dom would have no complaints about that case, I'm sure.

I sat down, and the lovely Sax showed me how to advance and rewind, gave me a pen and pad if I wanted to time code anything, and left me to it. I got to work.

It was fun watching everyone for the first fifteen minutes, spotting myself and some of my friends. Melanie and I met at our gym, so she wasn't present, or she would have been the video star, along with the few who always seemed to gravitate towards it. I saw Alex in the background a few times, hanging out with his usual group, except they all looked less geeky now that they were adult men. Several ladies from my class approached him and asked him to dance or just chatted. Well, you would; he was gorgeous.

After a while it got tediously boring and then, at last, I spotted Alex doing something interesting – he was standing near the exit and Angela was right, he was talking with Trent and Trad. I zoomed in like Sax showed me how to, and I noticed Trent was smiling and enjoying the talk, but Trad's expression was different. He appeared to be sizing up his competition. Then Trad and Alex grabbed their phones, and they looked like they were exchanging numbers. Five minutes later, they moved apart. Alex looked uncomfortable – he didn't fit in with his old group or this new fitness-conscious group. He was a fish out of water.

<center>~~~</center>

At dusk, I drove to the cliffs and the staircase where many people worked out to visit where Alex trained. Maybe I'd meet some people who trained with him. And by a lucky coincidence, Dom and a few of his fellow gym instructors were running drills there tonight. What a surprise... okay, I knew, call it good management. I loved watching Dom work out – it was so exhausting and satisfying; it made me feel like I, too, had a good session. Plus, it didn't hurt for the gym bunnies in his class to see he had a girlfriend, thank you very much. It's only a guess, but I thought Dom liked me to drop in now and then – I swear he worked out that bit harder and ensured I had a good show.

I parked at the top of the cliffs, and Atlas and I walked down the path, avoiding the stairs. We went for our daily walk for about forty minutes. I'd done the stair climb myself a few times but stopped doing them after Atlas halted midway once and wouldn't go any further. It forced me to carry him the rest of the way so we didn't block the stairs. Last time ever. A personal trainer who passed me at the top joked I'd have to carry a German Shepherd up next if I wanted to keep improving. Hilarious, once I got my breath back.

When we returned from our walk, Dom and his team were in action; he gave me a wave and smile and followed his team up the stairs – all 107 of them. Some of his group only did it once, then resorted to a light run and callisthenics nearby. Others did it multiple times, like Dom. I drifted away, thinking about Alex and the case, until I heard Dom finishing up, so I paid attention. He gave them all a rev-up and sent them off, then he came up the stairs again to us. He leaned down to kiss me; I put my hand on his chest.

'Yeah, no hugging, sweaty dude,' I said, and he laughed and rolled his eyes.

'There are girls out there who'd love a hug from a fit, handsome, sweaty dude,' he teased.

'Best you go find them then; we'll wait here,' I suggested, and he ignored me and patted Atlas instead.

'Let's walk so I can cool down,' he said, and we went along the top of the cliffs, looking down on the city and the river, beautiful and aglow in the dusk light. On our return, we stopped and looked over the edge.

'I asked around. Quite a few people remember Alex,' Dom said, 'the TV show promotion helped.'

'Ah, thanks for that. Did they see anything suspicious? You know, like someone giving him a hard time – a fellow contestant who was working out or a jealous partner?' I asked.

'I didn't ask that; it's a little hard to work that into the conversation,' Dom smiled.

'And you call yourself the partner of a private detective!' I teased him.

'One of my class said he always worked out with a girlfriend,' Dom added.

My eyes widened. 'Now you're talking. Anything else?'

'Nope.'

'Hmm,' I said, thinking. 'Girlfriend, huh? I'll add her to my suspect list.'

'You're welcome.' Dom grinned, lowering himself to sit on the rock fence and pulling me between his legs. Atlas sat, too, studying every dog and person passing by.

I gave him a grin but then went back to thinking out loud. 'I need to find this girl. I'll go to his gym and ask around.'

Dom looked worried and was just about to lecture me when I cut him off.

'Of course, if I discover anything worrying, I'll involve Officer Jason.'

'Right,' he said. 'I liked it much more when you were just publicising films and events.'

'Trust me,' I placed my hand on his chest, 'I'll be careful. Besides, there's been a few clients' publicity projects that I've nearly died of boredom promoting.'

'Not funny,' he said, unconvinced. 'Even though I didn't know him, Alex's death makes you want to grab every opportunity. You never know when your number is up.'

I nodded, knowing where he was going. 'You mean like dance like no one is watching, and all that.'

'Exactly. Thought any more about marrying me?' he asked and smiled. It was a romantic location, and I knew he was teasing and keeping it light-hearted, but he wasn't really. He wanted that, and I wasn't in any hurry for it. I don't get why everyone wanted to get married… there are so many who don't make it, like my parents, like me and my first husband – a big mistake.

'I've thought a lot about living happily ever after with you,' I said and kissed him. Then, I moved that conversation along. 'I got a small lead today; can I pick your brain?'

'All my body parts are available to you,' he said invitingly.

'Great. I'll take your brain for now and select a few other parts when we get home.' I told him about Alex's estranged wife, Lucy. Her online profile still said "married to Alex". I asked Dom: 'From your training experience, would you say it is pretty likely that if one partner got slim and the other didn't, the relationship was bound to fail?'

Dominic nodded. 'Yeah, I've seen it a few times. Often, couples will join the gym together, but one will drop out, and then in no time, the fit one is training with other people, dating and seeing someone else. But it's not always about body shape.'

'What is it about then?' I asked.

'It's the world that is opened up to them. Their lives can change – they're not interested in watching TV and getting a takeaway as much anymore. They want to go to the gym, do the Saturday morning 5km park runs, holiday with treks instead of cruises and bus tours, that sort of thing,' he said, 'and the new partner doesn't want that and never did. They just end up being different people.'

'Thanks, that makes sense.' I studied him for a moment. 'So, when we have Friday night takeaway and TV, are you privately thinking, *wish I was at the gym or trekking*?' I asked. 'Honest answer only!'

Dominic grinned. 'Trust me, I work out for a living every day of the week. I want to sit on the couch with you, and I don't care what we eat as long as we eat together.'

'So romantic,' I teased and kissed him.

'You're cold; let's go,' he said, pulling away as I shivered. Always the gentleman.

As we left, I looked back at the stairs, which Alex must have run up so many times, full of energy and with his new passion for life.

'Alex, such a waste,' I whispered. But I felt nothing. I was probably silly expecting to feel a presence... he was gone.

# Chapter 7

GABI, THE CHIEF PARTY Person, absolutely had to see me right this minute. She was one of those people who, when they decide to do something, must do it immediately. I was a bit like that myself, so I got it. She rang me on the way to the office, so I swung by her office instead. When I arrived, all her team was dutifully at their desks, looking at monitors and doing what they did.

'Oh good, you're here, excellent!' she exclaimed. 'Camille, can you please bring us tea in the Rose Room? You'll have tea, won't you, Jesse?'

'Please,' I said and smiled my thanks at Camille, who looked more like a work-experienced high school student than a slick event person like the rest of the team. Maybe that's how they all started.

I followed Gabi down the hallway, admiring her beautiful cream jacket, skirt, and insanely high heels. She stood aside to let me enter the meeting room first; I noticed she finished her outfit off with a fair bit of cleavage on show. The Rose Room was beautiful – rose wallpaper, red couches, a small meeting table with cream chairs and a large window that looked out onto a, yep, you guessed it, a rose garden. I imagine Gabi got help with the gardening as she didn't seem the green thumb type, and her nails were perfect.

'My dad does the gardening,' she said, reading my mind and seeing my admiration of the roses. 'Please take a seat. Jessica, I appreciate you coming so soon.'

'My pleasure, and actually it's just Jesse, that's truly what my mother christened me,' I told her and she smiled, then stared at my face.

'Jesse, Jesse, Jesse,' she said a few times, burning my face and name to memory. 'Got it!' she declared.

I sighed. 'If only that worked for me. I've forgotten my own name under pressure.'

Gabi laughed. She didn't ask if I found what I needed from my reunion video; I think Gabi worked very much in the now.

'I inherited this house,' she said, and I wasn't sure if we had started talking business now or not, but I paid attention regardless.

Gabi continued: 'Mum passed away two years ago with breast cancer, and I had been running my event business for the last five years from a rented space outside the city. So, I moved the business here, and Dad helped me set it up.'

I offered my condolences, and then Camille entered with a tray of tea and biscuits and left Gabi to serve. After pouring, she got back to her usual frantic self.

'I want to hire you, Jesse.'

'Great! To do what?' I asked, raising the delicate tea cup to sip the English Breakfast tea with milk and no sugar.

'To find my family's teddy bear.'

I almost spluttered my tea. *A bear? Seriously?* I placed the cup down again and tried to look serious. I was right; it was not Grandma's stolen cookie recipe, but it was near enough – I could see Dominic's look of delight already... no murderers, gangsters or thugs, just a teddy thief.

She held up her hand, her face serious. 'Before you think I'm having you on, or I'm giving you some fluffy case, let me explain,' she said, and I nodded for her to go on.

'My Grandma Ruby had her 80th birthday last weekend, and we organised a family reunion to celebrate it. We had it at Grandma and Grandad's place – they have a lovely big old home on the river at Chelmer. Probably about fifty or more of us were there, and only about ten of us remained to help clean up. The next day, Grandma rang Dad in a mad panic because T-Bear was missing.'

'Right. T-Bear stands for Teddy Bear?' I asked because one should not assume.

'No T-Bear stands for Titanic Bear. Have you heard of a Titanic Bear?' she asked.

*Had anyone?*

'No. What is it?' I asked, now super intrigued. I accepted a top-up of my tea. Gabi drank a few mouthfuls from her dainty cup before continuing.

'My Great-great-great Grandmother, Isabella, I think that's enough greats, whatever, it doesn't matter,' Gabi waved her hand in the air dismissing the thought, 'well she was on the Titanic with her mother and father.'

'Get out of here!' I said because I forgot myself for a moment.

'Incredible, but true. She survived ,but her parents didn't. G-G-G Isabella was 12 at the time and was shipped off, so to speak, to relatives. But a company gave her and other survivors a rare gift. Have you heard of the German company that makes teddy bears called Steiff?' she asked.

'Yes, oddly, I have!' I exclaimed, pleased with myself, and Gabi looked glad that I wasn't a total moron. I explained: 'One of my close friends worked for the Lagerfeld brand for a while, and Steiff made a Karl Lagerfeld teddy or a few thousand of them, I believe.'

'Yes! I bid on one of those but didn't get it,' Gabi said. 'Does your friend have one?'

'No. She wants one, but last time there was one up for auction, it went for $8000.'

Gabi shook her head in disbelief. 'Exactly. So, the Titanic Bear or T-Bear came into existence after the sinking of the Titanic in 1912. Steiff knew how comforting a teddy bear wa,s and they made 600 black teddy bears to mourn the victims. They called them the Titanic Mourning Bear. My G-G-G-Isabella was given one, and she loved it and guarded it all her life. It was all she had left to remind herself of her parents. In her will, she handed it down to the eldest daughter on the maternal side of the family. So, my Great Grandmother Audrey inherited T-Bear to look after. Now, Grandma Ruby, who just turned 80 and is still alive, is the custodian of T-Bear. Mum would have gotten it next if she had survived, but it would come to me after Grandma Ruby. Except someone stole it at the reunion.'

I gasped. 'No. How could they?'

'It's terrible,' Gabi agreed. 'Grandma Ruby is really upset because she feels she has let down her mother and grandmother. But what makes it worse is that they treat it as a big joke. Look at this.' Gabi grabbed her phone, thumbed through her photos, and showed them to me. It was an old black bear dangling from a jetty.

He had a beautiful face but now, knowing his history, he seemed such a sad little bear.

'Are they trying to be funny?' I asked, dismayed to see T-Bear treated so irreverently. 'Do you think you will get it back soon, and it will be a big joke?'

Gabi shook her head. 'I don't know. None of my family owns to having it, and the last photo I got...' she thumbed to a different shot, 'it looks like Sydney Harbour in the background... so T-Bear's left the state, but my relatives are still here. I haven't received a ransom note, and I'm worried that whoever has T-Bear will sell him; we've always thought T-bear was a boy.'

'Right. Is T-Bear insured?' I asked Gabi.

'Yes. I don't know how many are left in the world out of the 600 that were first made, but back in 2000, one of the Titanic Mourning Bears sold for $134,000.'

Again, I nearly fell off my chair. 'For a bear?' I exclaimed.

'Yes, but it's worth ten times that for Grandma.'

'Of course,' I said.

'I just have to check that Grandma Ruby is fine with me hiring you – I told her I was going to ask you – but will you take the case?'

'I will, thank you,' I said, then shared how I normally worked and the time spent, and we agreed on a rate and timeline. I promised not to mention it to anyone until she got back to me with the confirmation nod, but while I had her, I asked her for 15 concentrated minutes – I knew she would work well to a deadline. So, assuming I was getting the case, I pumped her on who was at her family reunion, when T-Bear was last seen in the house, who remained at that point and time, who might not want her to inherit, who might be in financial trouble, who was a joker, and who might have a grudge against her grandparents. I also got the guest list so I could crosscheck their social media accounts as soon as I got the green light and to make sure they hadn't left the state.

Apparently, T-Bear now has his own Instagram account. Someone must have set it up; I just had to find out who. But first, I had to swing by the office and pick up Ed. We had a meeting with our film client, Amanda.

# Chapter 8

I DIDN'T TELL ED about T-Bear just yet. I promised Gabi not to mention it to anyone until I got the green light and besides, Ed was cranky. He had not long been back in the office from his *Exotic Theatre* meeting and looked worse for wear. Meeting with our film client would cheer him up – Amanda was super laid back; her meetings were quick, and the film product was always interesting. Ed was waiting out the front of the office for me. I pulled up, and Ed jumped into the passenger seat, belted up, and shuddered.

'They're awful,' he said. 'I thought it would be so much fun promoting their play, but they fight over everything from where they want to stand for a photo, to who has the best lighting on them, to whether one of them delivered a line with too much panache. How would you say: *"He's so interesting"*?' Ed asked.

I repeated it back like I thought he was interesting.

Ed nodded. 'Yep, me too. But no, there was a twenty-minute discussion on whether they should emphasise the word *"so"* or *"interesting"*. I came this close to telling them they are all the least interesting people I have ever met!' he said, holding his finger and thumb really close together.

'But you keep it together!' I praised him.

He made a humph sound and kept talking. 'If their season is a hit and they get a second season, I'm resigning now. Thank God you're driving, I'm too stressed,' he said, exaggerating.

'Artists,' I said, shaking my head in sympathy.

'What time can we officially start cocktail hour without offending?' he asked with a glance at my car dashboard clock, and I chuckled. It was nearing 11am and our next meeting would take an hour.

'Well, after we visit Amanda, I have to go to the airport to see a flight attendant – I know, I'm very busy and important – and then drop in and see Mona at the choir's headquarters because she likes to see me now and then to ensure I'm still alive and working on her publicity. How about 4pm, on the couch, wine and pretzels? Bring a date, and I'll text Dom, Jason, and Mel. But if you need to start earlier...'

'I'll do my best to hold out,' he sighed melodramatically.

Tara Garner – a flight attendant for *Skip* Airlines – was hot, and she wasn't even my type. Tall with brown skin, wavy dark hair tied back and clasped at the back of her neck, and a heart-shaped face. She and Alex would have made a very cute couple.

'It was just a casual thing,' she said dismissively, ending that thought.

We sat opposite each other at the domestic terminal – she was on a flight departing for Cairns in forty minutes, and I needed to catch her while my case was fresh. And while I had nothing to go with, it seemed a good starting point. I wore a navy pantsuit and probably could have been mistaken for a flight attendant myself if I had a scarf on! I let Tara order the coffee; she got a staff discount.

'Obviously, you met him at work?' I asked, even though it was obvious, but you've got to check these things.

'Yes, a flight to Darwin with a couple of days overnighter on that occasion, that's when we first hitched up,' she said. 'All the crew stayed at the same hotel and ended up hanging out together. Alex and I just kept that going whenever we were away if neither of us was in a relationship,' Tara said. 'I guess all up, we've been casually seeing each other for a few months and hitched up about four times in that period.'

'Since he lost weight?' I asked.

She shrugged. 'I didn't see him before that. Maybe I didn't notice him, or maybe we hadn't been on any flights together. But after we hung out the first time, I discovered he was a contestant on that TV show. I saw the social media profile stuff they created for him.'

'He looks very different,' I said, understanding if she had not noticed him before.

Tara agreed. 'I couldn't believe it.' She looked away towards the departure board. 'I still think I will see him striding in here, looking amazing in his suit and hat. It hasn't sunk in yet.' Her bottom lip quivered, and she took a deep breath before returning her gaze to me.

'It is a shock,' I said sympathetically. 'I saw him only recently at our school reunion. He looked great,' I added.

'He was gorgeous,' she agreed, 'and he was respectful.'

'How?'

'He was nice, no ego. Some pilots think they are God's gift to the hosties, but Alex was so polite and caring. He'd help with luggage and little things like that and always ensured all the hosties got home safely if we were out partying while we were away. He was a gentleman, and a lot – and I mean a lot – of the girls really liked him, especially since he started the TV program.'

'Because he might win the prize money?' I asked.

She laughed like I was being silly. 'No, because of his profile. Alex had thousands of followers already on his online account, which the TV station created for him, and the show hasn't even gone to air yet. He was going to be hot property, and several of the girls thought it'd be great to get in early and enjoy the ride, so to speak. Some hosties would like to launch their modelling careers by being seen on his arm.'

'Oh, makes sense,' I said. *Good grief.* 'But you didn't love him?'

She shook her head. 'Neither of us felt that. But when he saw me on a flight, he was always pleased to see me and didn't ignore me. That was really nice, so we hitched up again. For me, I just never had that heart-stopping reaction. Do you know what I mean?'

I nodded, and we both sipped our coffees and thought about that while we waited for a boarding announcement to finish so we could be heard again.

'Do you have a partner?' Tara asked me.

'I do. Dominic, he's a personal trainer.'

'You lucky bitch,' she said and grinned.

I laughed. 'I know. He's easy to look at and puts no pressure on me to stay fit, although I'm conscious of it given the ladies he sees at his gym.'

'I get that,' she said. 'You'd have to be confident in yourself. Alex wasn't. Even as gorgeous as he was, he was unsure of himself. He could have had any girl he wanted, but he didn't play the field.'

'Maybe that's because he wasn't always gorgeous,' I said, thinking that might go some way towards explaining why. 'But he was quite outgoing at our reunion.'

'Oh yeah, he liked a good time; he just wasn't the leader of the pack,' she agreed. 'But...'

'But?'

'Nothing.'

I waited eagerly, and then she shook her head. 'No, it's wrong to speak ill of someone when they are not here to defend themselves.'

'Please, go on; it might help me understand what happened to him,' I prompted her. I wanted to grab Tara by the shoulders and shout, 'Tell me!' but I played it cool.

'Well, this is just my impression, but when we started hanging out together, he was really sweet. Maybe he'd never attracted women before, you know, never had female attention.'

I nodded my understanding, not speaking so she would carry on.

'But in the last month or so, there were so many women keen on him and really beautiful women too, that he got a bit full of himself. I think it didn't affect me because I didn't love him,' she said, contemplating what they had. 'But if I had been in love with him, I wonder if he would have been arrogant or dropped me when his dating pool was widening.'

'Hmm, that is a good observation. Thank you, Tara.'

'We'll never know though.'

'No, but given what you just said, can you think of anyone who didn't like him? Did he offend anyone, steal someone's girl, break a heart or slight anyone?'

Tara thought for a moment. 'It is possible that he broke a few hearts with his new look and profile, but if we killed pilots for doing that, there wouldn't be many left.'

We both laughed at her joke. Tara continued. 'I can ask around if you like... you know, subtly.'

'Brilliant, that would help, thank you.' I sounded desperate. I was. I had a cause of death that said he slipped down the television studio stairs, struck his head and died. That was it. It was clear cut, and I had a feeling I was just going to be going through the motions on this case and ticking boxes before I reported back to Alex's folks that I had nothing.

But then Tara changed that.

'There was one minor incident.'

I leaned forward, keen to hear this.

'It's probably got nothing to do with his death, but since you're asking....'

'I'm asking,' I agreed.

'His wife came to the airport just recently to meet him when he came off a flight.' She held up her hands in surrender. 'I promise you I didn't know he was married, and he told me later they were separated but not divorced. She was accusing all the hosties on his flight – including me – of sleeping with him and having no morals. He grabbed her arm and pulled her away. I kept going, so I don't know what happened, but it was super embarrassing,' Tara said.

I thought about Alex's wife, Lucy. Alex's father had mentioned that she had embarrassed Alex at work. Yet, it was odd that she was supposedly at the studio with him on his last day alive if they weren't a couple anymore. I didn't see her, not that I would have recognised Lucy that day I was there with Mel; Lucy hadn't come to the reunion. Was she with him on the stairwell when he fell? I gathered my thoughts and continued questioning Tara.

'And he never spoke of her, of Lucy?' I asked.

'Not even to say they were separated; I didn't know until I saw her that day.' Tara lowered her voice, 'I felt so sorry for her. She was a big girl and seemed insecure. Maybe that's why they split.' She glanced at her watch and reached for her bag. 'I really have to go.'

'I know and I'm grateful for your time, thanks Tara, you've been a great help.'

'Really? Anything for Alex. I'll message you if any of the girls come clean about sleeping with him or I get any other info.'

'Thank you, that's appreciated. And thanks for the coffee. I'm sorry for the loss of your friend, our Alex.'

'Me too,' she said and pouted.

We stood, and she hugged me. Huggy types... cute. That's why she's a flight attendant helping people and not an investigator annoying people. I walked a short distance with her to the escalator.

'I hope you can find out what happened if it wasn't an accident. It's such a waste,' she said with a departing wave.

I agreed and waved back as I got on the escalator, moving away from her. I felt the same; it was a colossal waste either way – if it was or wasn't an accident. So, Lucy, what is your story?

# Chapter 9

THE VISIT TO MONA took longer than I thought because she assumed I would want to stay for the choir's rehearsal. Of course, who wouldn't? Sigh. But it allowed me to get a few photos for social media. I chatted with several choristers to get some quirky media angles going should *Mahler's Symphony No.2* fail to excite the press. One chorister once performed with the successful violinist and showman André Rieu; another chorister's father was mayor many years ago. There are two angles I can flog to the entertainment editors.

I checked my phone while listening to the choir hit their notes, and there was a message from Gabi – I had the green light to run with T-Bear's case; she had attached the signed contract. Excellent, two cases on the go now!

Eventually, I escaped Mona's gig and returned to the office. I could hear laughter and voices as I stepped out of the elevator on my floor. At the same time, the accountant's door opened, and the middle-aged guy who ran the business exited. I held the lift for him. He was lanky and had a kind face.

'Early mark,' he explained.

'We're doing the same, but having a quiet drink. Would you like to join us?' I asked, being neighbourly.

He glanced down at my office door and looked tempted for a moment.

'I would if I didn't have a thing to attend tonight, hence the early mark. Next time?'

'For sure,' I said and farewelled him as the lift doors closed. He was probably not good for Mel. She worked with figures all day long; she didn't need to come home to an accountant. I know, I'm always thinking of my friends and how to get them hitched and off my back.

I opened the office door, and it was a full house for our small office – Ed and Simon, Melanie, Jason and even Dom were there.

'Here she is,' Dom said, getting up from the side of the couch where he was chatting with Mel. I saw his countenance relax. He didn't like me doing the private investigator work and assumed I was in constant danger. It will come to a head; I'm just waiting for it. Jason got up, too, and then sat back down. It was Dom's job to get me a drink, as boyfriend roles go.

I said hi to everyone and hugged Dom. He looked gorgeous, but he always did.

Ed's boyfriend Simon said: 'I'm loving this early-in-the-week happy hour idea, it's much better than waiting until Friday.' He came over to kiss me on the cheek, and I linked my arm through his as we made our way over to the couches.

'Ed is so grumpy with his clients of late,' I said, making sure Ed was in earshot, 'I hope he's not bringing that home with him.'

Ed gave me a smirk, and Simon rolled his eyes. 'A truer word has never been spoken. The sooner this theatre lot finishes, the happier we'll all be.'

'I'd be happier if Jesse were working on theatre clients instead of dangerous clients,' Dom said, handing me a glass of white wine. There it was again.

'If only,' Ed sighed dramatically. 'I'd handball those actors to her faster than you can say exit stage left.'

'There's an easy way to manage them,' Mel butted in, saving me from having to berate them both. We all turned to look at her expectantly.

'Name drop, Ed, name drop,' Mel said, sitting down and holding court. 'If you go in there and say... *At lunch recently with my favourite critic*" or "*The editor of blah blah rang me*", they are going to be kissing your butt so that you recommend them for interviews. Trust me,' she said.

Ed and I looked at each other and back at Mel.

'That's actually brilliant,' I said.

'Brilliant,' Ed echoed.

'I know,' she said and smiled. 'I used to be a theatre type.'

Then Officer Jason rose and checked out our whiteboard, which we should have closed in the middle before the happy hour guests arrived.

'Ah, you're looking into Alex Bryson's death? Poor guy. How did you score that?' he asked of the one case on my P.I. side of the board.

'Jess went to school with him,' Ed replied.

'Really?' Jason looked at me, wide-eyed with surprise. 'Good-looking guy.'

'Not back then,' I said and moving closer to the board, I pointed to Alex's school photos.

Jason ran a hand behind his neck as he studied the photos. 'It's going to be a tough call, that one,' he said, lowering his voice so only I could hear him. 'He slipped, hit his head, died. What are you hoping to find?'

I shrugged. 'That he was pushed. No,' I corrected myself, 'his parents hope I find it wasn't an accident so they can punish someone and try to make some sense of it. Understandable.'

'Yeah, sure is.' Jason nodded. 'Got any leads?'

'I might have one,' I said smugly.

'That so?' Jason grinned at me.

'Nuh, I've got nothing,' I confessed, and Jason chuckled. 'But I have another case that I'm about to put on the board; it's really exciting.'

We went to rejoin the group, and I was just about to tell them about T-Bear—the Titanic Mourning Bear—when the office door opened; I didn't even hear the lift. Trad, the jock from school, stood in the doorway… buffed, fit, and asking for me.

# Chapter 10

Every eye turned to look at Trad, and I rose. I handed my wine to Dom and headed to the door.

'Trad! Hi, would you like to come in and meet the team and have a drink,' I said politely. More politely than I felt because Trad was an ass at school, but I'm giving him the benefit of the doubt that he has improved with age. He certainly had in the looks department. He was cute at school, but now he was Chris Hemsworth, handsome and buffed. Not that I noticed because Dom's my type.

'Jesse, hi, I won't come in, but thanks. I just wanted to catch you for a moment, but I can come back another time,' he said, putting his hands in his jean pockets and looking sweet. If I turned around, I bet Mel's tongue would be out. I wasn't risking it.

'No, that's cool. Is it about Alex?' I asked, guessing it was the only reason he'd have to talk with me. I hadn't got to speak with him at the reunion, but that wasn't a big deal... there were a lot of people to catch up with.

'Yeah, but it's not urgent. Why don't you drop by my work when it suits you? I'm a trainer at Crossfit Gym and there every day.'

'Ah, Mel is a member there, aren't you, Mel?' I said, turning to involve her, and she was at my side faster than you could say 'cardio'.

'I am, hi, I'm Melanie.'

'Trad,' he said, offering his hand, and they mutually admired each other – blondes, fashionable, extrovert – the opposite to me.

'I do Kayla's morning classes a few days a week,' Mel continued.

'She's great, Kayla. Well, might see you there?' he said to her.

I broke into their stare-off. 'I'll drop in over the next few days,' I suggested, and Trad nodded.

'Sure, great, see you then,' and he headed out of the office. Mel continued to watch to make sure he got to the lift safely. I turned immediately and returned to the group.

'Who's that?' Ed asked because Dom and Jason probably wanted to but had to be diplomatic.

'That's Trad Hasler from school. I think he's been working out with Alex,' I said with a nod to our board, which should explain everything. 'I want to pick his brain.'

'Uh-huh,' Ed said, making it sound like there was more for the picking there if I wanted it. Dom had the slightly locked jaw thing going, and Jason was probably going to run Trad's profile when he returned to the station to see if Trad had a criminal record... he did ask me how to spell Trad's surname. They were both protective, which was sweet and annoying. I leapt in and changed the conversation – 'I might have another client, Gabi, Chief Party Person from *Party People*. How's that for a title?'

That worked, and the group was off on a tangent, talking about the best and worst titles they had ever encountered. Dom ran his hand up my back, and I looked up and smiled at him.

'Do you think somehow he was involved in Alex's death?' he asked me.

I bit my lip while thinking, then answered honestly. 'I don't know. But as they say in the crime shows, everyone's a suspect.'

'I can help interrogate him,' Mel said, arriving back next to me. I wish she and Jason had hit it off together. It's so hard being a matchmaker when your subjects don't take the bait. She then looked at her glass and noticed it was empty.

'Jace, let's get the second round going,' she said, and he rose to the occasion.

I wanted to get to my desk, check on my messages, and do some work since I had been out all day. It took another forty minutes of socialising before I could get rid of everyone, and I told Dom I'd see him at home. We both had cars here. Mel lingered, and I wanted her to do so. She'd helped in one of my earlier cases when a gorgeous blonde was required, and while I'd never put her in danger, I'm not above using the resources at hand.

'Need me?'

'Hell yeah,' I said, and we both grinned.

'At your service,' she said. 'What do you want me to do?'

'When you next do your gym workout, could you subtly – and I mean super subtly – sus out what the vibe is for Trad? You know, good guy, sweet, scary, troublesome, easily threatened by anyone else with potential?'

'Can do.' She smiled. Mel loved a mission.

'Thank you, Mel, you're a godsend,' I said, borrowing my school captain, Angela's line.

She kissed me on both cheeks. 'Later,' she said and headed off.

I sat at the desk, logged in and scanned emails. Just what I wanted... a message from the manager of Alex's gym telling me to drop in any time and he'd be happy to help. Right, add that to my list.

When I got home forty minutes later, Dominic was in the shower, so I called to him that Atlas and I were heading out for our walk. I quickly changed and grabbed Atty's lead, and we headed off – my favourite part of the day. We exchanged pleasantries – how much he had slept today and who went past our house. I told him about any dogs I saw, and then we enjoyed the cool dusk and passing the time of day with those we met, including regular neighbourhood dogs, Rex, a Labrador and Prudence, a French Bulldog. The walk gave me time to process information, chill out and unwind; I loved my quality time with Atlas.

Tomorrow was going to be a full-on day. Ed and I had to catch up on our water campaign, the solicitors' blog had to be drafted and sent back for sign-off, and I needed to prepare a few questions for Trad. I also wanted to follow up with Gabi and get the T-Bear case on the board and underway.

When we arrived home and entered the warmth of our lovely home, I was super impressed to see that Dominic had Atlas' dinner cut and served, and he had started cutting a stir-fry. I was even more impressed to find him shirtless while cutting the veggies, those abs on display and muscles flexing.

'Look at you go, thanks!' I said. Then I realised he had an ulterior motive. I think he wanted me to see his gym efforts were paying off and that Trad's muscles had nothing on his. I'm sure Dominic thought if I saw his naked chest and muscles glistening fresh from his shower, I would throw myself at him before we ate dinner.

He knew me so well.

*Chapter 11*

THE NEXT MORNING, I was office-bound, thank goodness, and Ed was late. I had visions of him having had an accident or his hairdryer breaking down, but I finally got a message from him saying he was on-site with a client – the temperamental group *Exotic Theatre*. He put an angry face emoji at the end of his message, so I'm guessing he wasn't ready to take the stage yet. I sent him a cheery message telling him to take his time and break a leg.

I put the T-Bear campaign up on the whiteboard. Seeing the studio black and white portrait photo of the small, blonde girl, just 12, in formal wear of the time, clutching a black bear was so macabre, but as Gabi said, great-great-great-grandmother Isabella found comfort from her Titanic Bear. The photo of T-Bear was equally dramatic – a large black bear with the sweetest face, worn by time.

The new case so absorbed me that I got a fright as Ed and Jason barged in together, laughing and breaking the silence.

'We met in the stairwell,' Ed explained.

'And about time you both got back to work and stopped having fun since I'm here keeping the economy afloat,' I teased them.

'Coffee?' Officer Jason Abingdon asked, handing me a takeaway from my favourite local café. It was my first for the morning, just what I needed.

'Yes, please!'

'And just like that, the economy goes on hold,' Ed teased.

It still gave me a bit of a fright when I saw a police officer in my office, and I'm guessing seeing him in uniform kept the other tenants on their feet. Carrying three coffees might be a giveaway that the visit was social.

I sipped my skinny cappuccino. 'So good, thank you, Jason. So, gentleman, what doin'?' I asked because I'm cool, and that's how Atlas and I talked to each other.

'Doin' a lot,' Jason said. 'I've got a hit and run, two break-ins, a domestic violence incident, and a cranky old girl who has had two garden gnomes stolen.'

'That'd make me cranky, too,' Ed agreed. We both looked at him. 'What? My father has two garden gnomes dressed in his football team colours. It's personal.'

'Right, better prioritise that case then,' I suggested to Jason, and he agreed. I sat on the edge of my desk as we all took a break and drank our coffees.

'Anyway, this is not a social call,' Jason said. 'I checked out your school friend who dropped in here at happy hour.'

I knew he would remember Trad's surname and the spelling from my brief mention. He's a cop and good on details.

Jason continued. 'The guy has had two warnings for fighting but no charges.'

'Thanks, Jace, that's great. What sort of fighting do you know?'

'Late night, alcohol-fuelled, street fighting.'

I nodded. That tells me nothing really except that he was a hothead; I'll store it away, you never know.

'I've got a new client,' I said. They both looked at me sceptically. 'It's a bear.'

Ed's mouth dropped open when he saw the photo of a black Teddy Bear stuck with heart-shaped magnets on my P.I. side of the board.

'Oh, you've made it,' he said. 'When you've been hired to find a teddy bear, that's the pinnacle. Dom must be thrilled,' he said with a grin. 'Much more *bear*able than cheating partners and sabotaged cars.'

'I know,' I agreed sunnily, 'I think this might be my best one yet and the most *paw*-sible for success.'

'I bet you'll *bare*ly notice the difference – a shifty bear, a thief, a thug, all the same,' Jason said and grinned.

'They'll be *polar* opposites,' I assured him. We could do this all day – Ed and I often did until one of us ran out of puns; the winner was the last one punning.

Ed studied me to see if I was serious about my new bear job. 'Is that what you are doing, though, really? Finding a bear and a motley-looking one at that?'

'Yeah, what did the bear do? Was he *bear*ing arms? He looks shifty and thread*bare*,' Jason said, peppering me with more bad bear puns while accepting a shortbread biscuit from Ed's tinned supply.

'The bear's the victim,' I said. 'This is serious.'

'Stop, stop,' Ed said, 'this is too good. We have to sit down with our coffees and biscuits, then you can continue.' Ed liked ceremony.

I gave him a smirk but took a biscuit from the tin. They were the best shortbread I'd ever tasted. Once they were both seated, Ed, with his feet on his desk, allowed me to proceed.

'It's a Titanic Mourning Bear.'

Ed's eyes widened. 'No! Is that a thing? What is that?'

I told them all about it, and neither of them had heard of the bears or their maker, which made me feel better that I wasn't completely out of touch with the rest of the world.

'That's amazing!' Ed said when I finished.

'I know.'

'Wow,' Jason added.

'That's what I said,' I agreed and admired the photo of beautiful young Isabella as we finished our coffee and biscuits. 'I need to talk to a tech person to see if they can trace the person who opened T-Bear's Instagram account, then I've got my bear thief!'

Jason grimaced.

'What? You don't want to save the bear?' I asked.

Ed looked shocked. 'Oh, I couldn't *bear* it if you didn't want to save the bear, Officer Jason. If saving Teddy is not a priority, you've been in the job too long.'

Jason grinned. 'I want to save the bear, trust me – I'm not a complete bar-*bear*-ian,' he said. We groaned as expected. 'But,' Jason sobered, 'the chances of tracing the account owner are slim. Surely, the bear thief would have used a false name and set it up on a burner phone.'

I sighed. 'I know, but it's the first place to start.'

'If you're lucky, they might not be very smart,' Ed agreed.

'They've stolen a bear worth $130,000 from under everyone's nose. I'm guessing they are cluey,' I told them.

Jason choked on his coffee. When he could speak again, he asked: 'No, $130,000?'

I nodded.

'You might catch them if you could get them to send a self *paw*-trait,' Ed suggested and laughed.

I indulged him that it was a good one. Then, I turned back to the whiteboard. 'I'll have to talk with every family member who came to Gabi's grandma's birthday reunion,' I sighed, 'there'll be a *bare*-face liar amongst them somewhere!' I glanced at Ed for his rating on that pun; he gave me a thumbs-up.

'It will require patient for*bear*ance,' Ed agreed.

I was thinking of letting him win. It was becoming un*bear*able coming up with bear puns.

'I'd better get going,' Jason said. 'If you want to bounce anything off me or if you find anything...'

'Or when she needs you to look up something for her,' Ed added, and I gave him a *'whose side are you on'* look, which just made him laugh.

'Always happy to share my information with the boys and girls in blue,' I said charitably, 'and thanks for the coffee.'

'Anytime. I promise I'll get onto those stolen garden gnomes. Warn your dad, Ed, someone's collecting them.' He was gone in minutes.

Ed grabbed his phone to call his dad. Ah, weird world, missing gnomes and bears, dead reality stars, sunken ships....

When we heard the lift go, Ed glanced at me: 'You know he's still hot for you.'

'Nuh, he's over that.'

'He's not. He'd come here every day if he could find an excuse.'

'We're just friends,' I said and shrugged.

'But if you weren't going out with Dom, trust me, Jason would be right on the scene. You could do worse.'

I knew it. Jason was fun, good-looking and kind. Plus, he was going places and was bound to be a detective in no time. But my heart remained firmly with Dom.

'I'm enjoying my day in the office,' I announced, changing the subject. 'Next, I'm going to work on Mona's choir account. I'm almost looking forward to it.'

Ed shook his head. '*Fur* the love of God, no one is buying that.'

# Chapter 12

Melanie came for dinner. Dominic worked back late at the gym one night a week running classes, so to support his efforts, Mel and I sat on the couch, drank wine, ate a takeaway, or I threw together a quick nachos dinner, which I did tonight. With panache seen only in the best kitchens, I added the lemon to my guacamole, stirred it, and announced it was done.

It was easy to tell when Mel visited… there was usually a trail of items from the door, including shoes, jackets, keys, bags, folders… you just have to follow it in reverse on her way out to ensure she leaves nothing behind.

Mel grinned. 'I have very interesting news about Trad.'

'Uh-huh, do tell!' I said, giving Mel my full attention. She was an actress at heart, so I knew she'd enjoy having the stage.

'People love to talk,' she said, surprised. It surprised me this came from Mel, the talker. She took a sip of her wine and began. 'I casually mentioned Alex, and the *Lose it!* TV show in the changing room with some girls before our workout, and the girls were really into the subject. One of them told me that several gym instructors had auditioned to be on the show as fitness trainers but didn't get the gig.'

'I wonder if Trad auditioned?' I asked.

'I don't know, and I couldn't get that information, but then I caught up with Kayla, my CrossFit gym instructor, just before the class. I asked her if she had tried out or knew who had, and she said no but that the producers kept a shortlist so you could still have a chance down the track. Then she added those things were all about who you knew to get you in the door.'

'Interesting,' I said. 'Trad had an insider, his new friend, Alex, whom he'd never given the time of day to before, mind you.'

'Hmm,' Mel said, stopping to sip her wine while I thought about how Alex could have shortcut that for Trad if he introduced him to the TV crew and to the right people.

Mel continued. 'I casually mentioned I had met Trad.'

'How did she react when you said his name?' I asked.

Mel made a face. 'Like that.'

'Ah,' I said, studying her. 'So that's a face that says *I'm not a big fan of Trad*?'

'Yeah. I thought it was a *"been there, had him and got the scars to prove it"* face. He is pretty gorgeous so I suspect if he's single, he'd be working his way through the instructors.'

'What's Kayla like?' I asked.

'Lovely, fit, a good body, about your height, pretty, not beautiful, not overly confident, but open and friendly,' Mel said. She'd given that some thought, I suspect, while sizing up her chances with Trad.

'Did she say much about Trad, you know… he was an ex, or they had a fling?'

'No, but she said he trains for triathlons because he hopes the more wins he can get under his belt, the more appealing he'll be for a TV role and the bigger his following will be!'

I leaned over for a handful of pretzels and encouraged Mel to go on.

'Kayla also said Trad's girlfriend trained for the female sections of various triathlons and trains at the cliffs, where Alex trained.'

'Trad's girlfriend was training at the same place as Alex?' I asked. 'They must have seen each other or met. Strange coincidence.' My eyes narrowed – it happened when I was thinking suspicious thoughts. 'When I was at the cliffs the other night with Dom, it seemed pretty intimate. You'd probably get to know the same people if you regularly train there.'

Mel pursed her lips as she thought. 'I wonder if they trained together and Trad heard about it and didn't like it or if he saw them working out together.'

'I don't think so because Trad and Trent looked surprised to see a fit Alex in the footage I've seen from our reunion. If they'd seen him before the reunion at training, surely they would have exchanged phone numbers then not at the reunion.'

Mel agreed.

'Your information is brilliant, and later, when I'm not under the influence, I'll process it,' I said. 'Perhaps you had better avoid Trad altogether if you see him around the gym, Mel, just in case he is a bit unhinged.'

She frowned. 'It's a big call to think Trad bumped off Alex because he was training with Trad's girlfriend at the cliffs,' Mel said. 'And besides, he's hot.'

'Yeah, well, that's true,' I said. But just how egotistical was Trad, and how much of a threat was Alex with his rising media profile and interest in Trad's girlfriend? I think Trad's best friend, Trent, was just the person to tell me.

I didn't sleep. It started when a phone message woke me up just after 11pm. I grabbed it, thinking of all the bad things that could happen at that hour of the night and who might message me to tell me about them. But it was Gabi, Chief Party Person, forwarding me the photo she had just received of T-Bear being dangled in the Yarra River in Melbourne. He was getting around; in the last photo I received from Gabi, he was in Sydney. I messaged I'd call her in the morning and that I had a plan. I'd have one by then, hopefully.

I thought about it overnight, for hours on end. Next to me, Dominic slept the sleep of the dead. In the early hours of the morning, while I tossed and turned with visions of Alex at school and T-Bear being held for ransom, it came to me – what to do. I wanted to run it by Ed first because I was sleep-deprived, and then I'd talk with Gabi after getting Ed's input. It was the first time that the P.I. and the publicity business came together, which would also help Gabi's business. I breathed out and relaxed for the first time since my head hit the pillow and then my alarm went off. Bummer.

# Chapter 13

AFTER A MORNING RUN with Atlas, I went straight to the gym to meet Trad. He must have spotted me at reception before I even asked for him and he lobbed beside me. He might be fit and look hot in his gym gear, but it was still Trad Hasler from school... and he was an ass then, and probably still was an ass.

'Jesse, good to see you. Come through and we'll talk,' he said, nodding towards the weight section which must be his 'office'.

I thanked the receptionist anyway and followed.

'Hey, thanks for dropping into the office. Did you hear that Alex's parents have asked me to look into his death?' I said and cut to the chase.

'Yeah, and I wanted to let you know my girlfriend met him while she was training.'

Damn! I was hoping to catch him out in a lie that he didn't know they knew each other. But does he know if they trained together? Would Trad's girlfriend admit that to him or water it down in her admission to him?

He pointed to a weights bench and I sat down. Trad sat on one opposite and continued. 'Casey —— that's my girlfriend — she's in training for the Trans-triathlon and saw Alex training at the cliff stairs. When we saw the news reports, she said that she'd seen him training there. Casey couldn't believe we went to school together. I showed her the school photo of Alex; it blew her away. Amazing, huh?'

'I know,' I agreed. 'It took me by surprise too when I saw him at the reunion and then heard about his death. He had undergone an amazing transformation, though.'

'It's his parent's fault. They've overfed him for years, poor guy,' he said in a rare show of kindness for what I remembered of Trad. Perhaps I needed to rethink my position on him. Maybe he was a self-reformed ass.

'Did you ever train with him?' I asked, hopeful that I could pin him on the cliffs with Alex.

'No. I'm not into the cliff stairs. They're boring. Trent and I train on landscapes... you know, we pick an area similar to the triathlon landscape we are going to take part in. That works better. Most of our weekends have been on location doing that.'

'Right. Did your girlfriend say much about Alex, anything useful?' I asked.

Trad shrugged. 'Nothing memorable. I don't think she met him, just saw him while she was training, said hello, that sort of thing. A hell of a lot of people train there.'

'That's true,' I agreed.

'I wish I'd known Alex had found his fitness and was training; he could have worked out with us,' he said.

I smiled at him fondly for old time's sake. I wasn't buying a word of it.

⁓ℓℓ⁓

From Trad's gym, I went straight to Alex's gym – was I becoming what they call a gym junkie? Nah, probably not, I think that requires you to workout. When I arrived, the manager was doing his own workout – weights. He gave me a hand signal that he would be five more minutes. I nodded and smiled my encouragement. I'm the last person in the world to want to stop a shirtless man lifting weights in a gym when it was clearly so good for his health.

I was studying the notices on their board when he arrived beside me.

'Zac,' he said, wiping his hand on a towel and offering it to me to shake. 'Sorry to hold you up.'

'No, you didn't at all. I came unannounced,' I said charmingly because that's me.

He motioned to some chairs and tables in an open area and he grabbed two bottles of water — one for me and one for him — and we sat. I told him why I was asking about Alex and got to the point.

'Alex, right,' he said, thinking. 'I have to be honest with you. When I got your note, I had to look up who he was. We have about 200 members and the *Lose it!* team paid for his membership but he didn't come here much.'

'Oh! So he wasn't obliged to do set hours here as part of his TV contract or anything like that?' I asked, surprised.

Zac shook his head. 'Nope. The contestants can exercise how they like and when they like as long as they lose weight. *Lose it!* provide the membership to encourage them, but Alex wasn't big on the gym, I don't think. Hold up,' he said and turned to look around. He yelled out, 'Tino, got a minute?'

Tino stopped his weight session and came over.

'Tino's an instructor here too,' he said by way of introduction. We greeted each other and Zac continued: 'Jesse here is asking about Alex. You know, the *Lose it!* guy? Do you remember much about him?'

Tino shook his head. 'He didn't like the gym, just wasn't comfortable here, I'd say. I gave him one-on-one sessions where he didn't have to compare himself to others, but he thanked me and said he preferred to exercise outdoors.'

'Right. So did he make friends with anyone, guys or girls?'

Tino shook his head. 'I reckon he was here two or three times max, wouldn't you say Zac? I'll get our receptionist to check it out because his membership card would have logged him in.'

'That would be great, thanks. I'll come with you and leave you to get back to it, Zac. Thanks for your time.'

'Sure,' he said, and we shook again. Tino was right. Alex visited the gym a few times and then didn't return. Mustn't have been his scene. Well, nothing to gain from the gym, but at least it was off the list. Back to the office and to Ed, who was nothing like the gym folk, and that was a good thing. After all, how much gym can any one girl take?

# Chapter 14

ED LOVED MY PLAN, he agreed it had legs and paws, or in his words, was paw-some! I rang Gabi and asked if she would come to see us in our office as soon as possible this morning. In the meantime, I spent the remaining morning hours entirely on her case. I had the list of the ten relatives that stayed behind to help clean up at Grandma Ruby's 80th birthday celebration and reunion when Gabi had last seen T-Bear on the mantlepiece where he normally sat.

I worked through them, avoiding their mobiles... they could be anywhere in the country on a mobile. I wanted to know if they were home and could not be on the road with T-Bear. I called their place of work, and if they answered, I introduced myself, told them I was working on the case, and asked if they could share any information that might help me. The relatives I reached were very obliging.

If they didn't answer, I spoke to someone in their office and asked where they were and if I could make an appointment to see them today. I didn't intend to book the appointment;

I just wanted to know if they were local. I found six were at home or in the office locally; three relatives were not available when I called, but I could get appointments with them today, so the odds were they were still local, and one rang me back twenty minutes later and offered to meet me later in the day if I wanted, I didn't. They were all in the clear. Damn it. It was a good result and a bad one too – it meant none of the ten people present was in Melbourne with T-Bear. Bummer.

It was time to roll out my plan, and not a moment too soon – I heard the lift door open, and moments later, Gabi knocked and swanned in, looking amazing like she was heading off to an event herself, not just managing them. Today, she was in a stylish black dress with a full skirt finishing just above the knees and killer heels. Her hair was out and long, blonde and wavy, and she was carrying three coffees.

'I never meet my clients without a coffee hit, so I thought I'd extend the courtesy,' she said, charming us both. I invited her to sit at our large meeting table. Ed joined us because this would be a joint campaign now if Gabi agreed.

'Thank you, wonderful,' I said, accepting the latte. It wasn't usually my choice of coffee, but who cares? It's coffee that is free and hot.

Gabi knew how to work a room; she was charming and won Ed over in the first few minutes, but she had him at latte.

I began. 'So, I have an idea for you. As you may know, I also run a publicity agency.'

'I know,' she said. 'I've checked you out. You have some good clients.'

We nodded. 'They're loyal, thank goodness. But to T-Bear... because it is such a unique case and T-Bear is exceptional, I have an idea on how we could harness the goodwill of the community to want to find him, whet the media's appetite with the amazing Titanic story, ensure T-Bear is difficult to sell because he'll have a "stolen bear" profile, and a side-benefit would be potential interviews with you and for your business, if you did the interviews in front of your office signage.'

She sat back, and her eyes widened with interest. 'I am loving this, please go on.'

'Okay. We run a *Missing Bear* campaign.'

Gabi laughed out loud. 'Yes!'

I smiled and kept going: 'We use social media to put out a missing bear notice. Ed will write a media release about the Titanic Mourning Bear, his significance to the family, and the fact that someone has kidnapped him. All media interviews will go directly to you – Gabi Gordon from *Party People*, a descendant of a Titanic survivor and carer-to-be of T-Bear.'

'Oh my God, this is so good,' Gabi gushed and clapped her hands.

I kept going. 'We will create MISSING posters with a tear-away fringe where people tear off a scrap of paper with the website listed to report sightings. The distribution company we use for letterbox campaigns can put them up for us on power poles in Melbourne, Sydney, and Brisbane inner city areas. They're cheap, so we're looking at a few hundred dollars at most.'

'It can come out of my marketing budget,' Gabi said, understanding how the publicity would work for her.

'We will need staff to monitor the sightings that come in, assuming we get sightings, and then to send us anything that they believe might be a genuine lead. We'll ask the public to check their CCTV footage, phones, dash cam... it's amazing what people photograph and record.'

'No problem, I have my team and heaps of bright work experience students we can use,' she said. 'It will be a good assignment for their CVs too!'

'Perfect. We need an incentive other than compassion and being the person who brings T-Bear home... a small reward and it doesn't have to be much, but—'

Gabi cut me off. 'That's no problem. Grandma Ruby already offered to put up a reward of $10,000.'

'Fantastic!' I said enthusiastically and grinned at Ed. Our plan was coming together.

'Why don't we split it up to create more interest in the prize?' Ed suggested, 'What if we offer $6000 to whoever provides information that leads to bringing T-Bear home and two lots of $2000 for genuine information that contributed to finding T-Bear along the way at the discretion of T-Bear's carer, Gabi?'

'I'm good with that,' Gabi said.

'Great, me too,' I said.

'Oh, I love it, it's brilliant,' she said, her eyes alight with enthusiasm. 'Let's say no questions asked for his safe return.'

'Done,' I told Gabi. 'The other benefit of the campaign is that it ensures the bear is difficult to sell... traders will recognise this is the bear in the media and may call the police if T-Bear's captor tries to sell him.'

'Jesse, Ed, I love it. How soon can we roll it out?'

'As soon as your social media manager can set up a *"Find T-Bear"* page with photos, history, real-time traffic, and search information, it can link to your website, and that will save us time getting domains, outlaying for hosting, and it will bring you hits to your page.'

Ed told Gabi: 'I'll have the press release done within an hour.'

Gabi clapped her hands together. 'I'll tell Raj, my social media guru, to drop everything and get onto it.'

'So, off with the *paws* button and hit play, let's get to work!' I said.

I couldn't help myself. Hang in there, T-Bear; we'll be bringing you home any day now.

# Chapter 15

I ALWAYS LIKED TRENT more than I liked Trad – not much more because they were both inseparable pains-in-the-butt at school, but Trent was nice on his own. When he got with Trad, it was like he had to be obnoxious.

I got the T-Bear campaign underway, and Raj and Ed were confident they'd be right to push the launch button at 3pm this afternoon as agreed. Now I was changing hats and going to catch up with Trent. It's a good thing I enjoyed being busy. Entering the school grounds, I felt like a fish out of water – Trent was a physical education teacher at an all-boys school and had returned my request to see him with a lunchtime invitation. I told him I'd bring the sandwiches and drinks, and I did – egg and lettuce for both of us, a Diet Coke for me, and juice for Trent. I didn't make them; that would be ridiculous, especially when the nearby deli made the best fresh sandwiches.

'Much better than the tuckshop,' he said after a mouthful. 'Thanks.'

'Pleasure. Thanks for seeing me. Got many female teachers?' I asked.

'Yep, but they're all mature age. It's less of a distraction with a school full of young men fuelled by testosterone.'

I agreed. 'I crushed on all my male teachers... they were the first men I'd known aside from Dad.'

Trent grinned. 'I was in love with Ms Keeper, our history teacher. It ended up being my best subject after sport.'

I laughed as we sat on a deck overlooking the playing field where Trent conducted most of his classes. He had some of his students playing a casual football game, and now and then, he'd yell an instruction. Two boys walked past and teased him.

'Hello, Miss. Is this your girlfriend, Mr Turner?' one boy asked and grinned.

'If she were Thomas, you'd be the first to know,' he retorted, and the boys laughed and walked on. 'Makes me regret the hard time I gave all my teachers,' he said, shaking his head.

'Really?' I asked, 'because you were bad, I remember.'

'Get out.' He turned to grin at me. He had a boyish grin; I might even like him in another time and in another world where Trad didn't exist.

After some more sandwiches and small talk, I got down to business.

'So, can we talk about Alex?' I asked.

'Sure,' he said. 'To be honest, I didn't really know Alex. I never gave him a moment's thought at school, and truth be told, I gave him a hard time. Or Trad did, and I went along with it. When I see that happening now to some of my students, I feel so bloody bad for them, and here I was, the instigator in my school days.'

'We've all done things we're not proud of, I'm sure.'

'Yeah?' He smiled. 'Bet you haven't.'

'Have to,' I assured him. Then shrugged. 'I wouldn't get arrested for it, but you know, I broke a few hearts and could have been kinder. I could have stuck up for some friends, but I was too much of a follower. That sort of thing.'

'Yeah,' he agreed, 'I know all about being a follower.'

It surprised me that Trent admitted to that; it was fairly gutsy of him. I cut to the chase.

'Trad said he never saw Alex at the cliffs and that neither of you train there. He mentioned his girlfriend saw Alex training but barely knew him. Is that how you remember it? Is that your relationship with Alex, too?'

Trent nodded. 'Pretty much.'

'So, the first time you saw Alex again since school was at the reunion?' I asked.

'Yep,' he answered. 'Wouldn't have recognised him if we'd passed in the street.'

Fair enough. I had the feeling Trent was holding out, but why? I shut up for a moment and let him stew in silence. A couple of his students went past and checked us both out. I looked to Trent, and he gave a small shrug and said: 'We heard from Trad's girlfriend, Casey, that a guy who got accepted for *Lose It!* was training at the cliffs. Trad and I didn't know it was Alex, then.'

I tried to play it cool.

'Casey must have spoken with Alex then to know that, or I guess she could have just heard about it from others when they were both training at the cliffs.'

'Yeah, maybe,' he said.

'And you exchanged numbers at the reunion. Was that so you could train together?' I asked.

'I didn't. Only Trad and Alex swapped numbers.' He ran his tongue over his lower lip in a nervous gesture. 'Trad is trying to raise his profile as a personal trainer; he wants to go out on his own, develop his own brand, you know that sort of thing.'

'Ah, right,' I said, a picture formed in my mind. 'Has he got a reasonable online presence?'

'It's growing, but he wants it to get bigger. I couldn't give a toss about that sort of thing, and my students would give me hell if I started posing online.' He laughed at the thought. 'Don't tell Trad I told you, but he thought connecting with Alex might help him. Alex's profile on the *Lose it!* site was huge, and Trad thought if he could train with Alex, he could get himself featured in Alex's social media feed.'

The school bell rang, and we both rose – old habits die hard.

'Must be weird hearing that every day,' I said.

'It's weirder getting up in the morning to get ready for school,' he joked.

'Thanks for helping me. One last quick question,' I said as we walked back to the main building, 'is Trad ambitious enough to get what he wants at all costs?'

Trent looked at me and thought about the question for a few moments. 'Let's just say we've always got on because I'm not competitive.'

When I got back to the office around four o'clock, everything was going off in a good way.

'Eight interview requests already since we launched the campaign over an hour ago,' Ed said before I had even put my bag down. 'Gabi's thrilled; we should have charged her a PR fee.'

'It crossed my mind,' I said, 'but it had better lead to finding T-Bear since that's the mission.'

'This might just be the best campaign we've ever "not" done for a PR client – its been shared thousands of times and gone absolutely viral.'

I grinned and sunk into my office chair. 'If only all our clients or my cases got as much traction.'

'We'd be going for long lunches every day and finishing early,' he agreed.

'We'd soon get bored with that,' I said.

'For sure,' he agreed, and we looked at each other like neither of us truly believed that for one moment.

# Chapter 16

I braced myself for Dominic's return from his family dinner this evening. It was unfortunate that I had to work... who am I kidding? I'd do anything to get out of going. If Dom wasn't the centre of attention for the night, everything was fine – so the bigger the group, the safer I was. I silently prayed that all his sisters, their husbands, and kids were in town and went along. But if it was a small group or his family decided it was time to focus on Dom's life and share their advice for how it should go, he would come home restless and wondering if we wanted the same things.

We didn't, not yet.

Maybe it was time I agreed to get engaged just so he could have the security he wanted. Even if it wasn't what I wanted yet. Melanie always reminded me I could have a very long engagement, but I thought it would just increase the pressure to get married.

I was in bed reading when Dom came in. After he had showered, he climbed in beside me. I put my book down and adjusted the light so it wasn't shining on us like a Spanish Inquisition.

'How's your Mum?'

'Good, she sends her best.'

'And your sister, sister, sister, sister, and other sister?' I asked, reflecting on poor Mr Darcy in *Pride and Prejudice,* enquiring after Miss Elizabeth Bennett's large family. Dominic had plenty of sisters to share around.

Dom grinned. 'Good, and before you ask, their partners and kids are good too.'

'Excellent,' I leaned over and kissed him, buoyed because it seemed like they were all present, and I might be off the hook. But no, he stopped after one kiss, which was unusual, except on monthly family dinner night. Yep, waiting for it...

'I've made a decision,' he said.

*And there it was. Stay calm, deep breath.*

'What's that?' I asked, feigning interest when I didn't want to know because I could put money on what he would say. My book suddenly had much more appeal.

'I'm going to try for a job as a consultant fitness adviser or personal trainer on *Lose it!'* He held up his hand to stop me from saying anything and continued. 'They'd be inundated with applicants, I know, but I might get a look in with the nutrition and lecturing work I've been doing, along with the personal training. If not, I'll ask if I can volunteer and watch on set, then I can be your inside guy.'

I think my mouth dropped open. I wasn't expecting that, not in all the scenarios I had prepared for in my head. What the hell?

'Why?' I turned side-on to face him and to delve into where this idea came from.

He sat back, adjusting a pillow behind him, all his perfect abs on display – so distracting, damn him.

'I was thinking about my role in the family when I was sitting there tonight, listening to all the banter. With four of my sisters married now, it just leaves Mum and Bianca. She's turning 21 in a few months and is the only one I have to look out for now.'

'That's so nice of you,' I said. Dom was always the gentleman and the head of the family by default since his father wasn't around. 'I wish I had a brother.'

'You have me, and if you are going to put yourself in danger by finding out what happened to Alex – if it wasn't an accident – then I'm going to be on hand to protect you.'

I studied him.

'What?' he asked.

'Then you will be in more danger than I might be. You could get pushed down the stairs or mugged on the set!'

'Exactly. But at least I'd be there while you are investigating, and you would know for sure then that there was more to Alex's death.' He crossed his arms over his chest, showing off his spectacular muscles. I should make him wear a shirt when we're having serious discussions. It's distracting and unfair.

I thought about what he said for a few moments – it took me longer because of his muscles – meanwhile, he stared at me, waiting for my decision. I turned and laid down on my back, fully aware of what he was playing at, but I let him think he was getting away with it for a short while, and then I ended that.

'Nah, that's a dumb idea,' I said, 'but thanks anyway.'

He burst out laughing and grabbed me, attempting to tickle me, which he knows I hate with a passion.

'No, it's not happening,' I said, pushing him away, and he stopped and sighed.

As quick as a flash, I straddled him. Unlike Dominic, I had some clothes on above the waist – a singlet and matching pants.

'I appreciate it, I do, but I know what you are doing,' I told him, webbing my fingers through his and holding him down with my weight – pointless, really.

'I'm undressing you,' he said, easily getting free.

I stopped him from going further, intending to thrash this out, so to speak, before we got hot and heavy.

'I know what you are doing and why,' I continued. 'You don't like me doing this line of work, I know, I get it.'

He put his hands on my waist and waited. I continued.

'You think if you put yourself in a similar situation, I will see how awful it is for the other partner, come to my senses, and let the business go.' His jaw locked. 'But all you are doing, Dom, is distracting me so that I'm off my game and not watching out for my safety because I'm worried about you. It's a mutual thing... guys want to protect; girls want to nurture and keep their loved ones safe too.'

He interrupted me, but I stopped him. He would not win this one, and I would not talk about it all night.

'I appreciate it, but it is not what I need from you. I've been working all night, and what I could use from my guy is something to relax me so I can sleep.' I smiled at him. 'Any ideas, coach?'

He rolled his eyes at me and gave the smallest smile. Then he began the serious business of running his hands up from my waist under my singlet.

I've always been good at delegating.

# Chapter 17

I WAS PLEASED TO be out of there – visiting bereaved clients was the hardest gig, and Alex's parents were totally invested in his life and death. Understandably, especially as he was their only child. They were looking to start a foundation in his name and meeting with bereaved parent groups – I imagine it helped to harness their grief and gave them a reason to get up in the morning.

Their riverside apartment on the tenth floor in West End was amazing, but not for me. I liked the lower floors where I could see the action – boats on the river, joggers on the track, cyclists, walkers, dogs, life in motion – all the energy of the day. Those lower units were always cheaper, too, a happy coincidence.

Driving out of their car park en route to my office, I thought about this morning's meeting: Jenny offered me tea or coffee, but I wanted to fast-track it out of there, so I declined. We sat, and I gave them an update, but I wanted to be selective in what I told them since Gary was a hothead. I began: 'An old acquaintance from school interests me... he's competitive, and I think Alex knew his girlfriend. It might be nothing, but I want to exhaust it.'

'Who is it?' Gary asked.

'I can't tell you that.' He was about to go off again, but I stopped him. 'It could be nothing, and I have to protect him and you.' He made a huffing sound, and I continued. 'The producer also allowed me to interview competitors on the *Lose it!* show. I don't think there's any chance that anyone amongst that lot deliberately harmed Alex to move higher up the ladder.'

Jenny nodded. 'Thanks, Jesse, that's great. You are doing a good job.' She glanced at her husband.

'Alex's phone and email records revealed nothing out of the ordinary,' I said without flagging the new relationship with Trad. 'I'd like to continue for another week while I pursue a few loose ends, then we can review if it is worth my continuing. Does that seem fair to you and your budget?' I asked and rose to leave.

'Absolutely,' Jenny said, rising to see me out.

'Budget is not a problem,' Gary said. 'We want to find out what happened to our son, but we don't want it dragging on, so you know if you can't find anything more or can't reveal—'

'Gary!' Jenny snapped at him. 'I'm sorry,' she said, turning to me and exhaling.

I gave her a warm smile and turned to her husband.

'That is your prerogative, Gary, and I'll hand over whatever I have found to anyone else you wish to appoint. So we'll talk next week unless I have information sooner.'

Gary returned to the couch and sank onto it.

'Jesse, I apologise,' he said again. 'I'm just so...' he put his head back on the couch and sighed.

'Angry, frustrated, helpless?' I offered.

'Yeah,' he agreed.

'There is something you can do to help me.' I threw him a bone; giving him a safe project might distract his energies.

'Anything.' He sat forward again; his eyes widened with interest.

'It won't be easy to do,' I said.

'That's okay, we'll do anything to help,' he said, and Jenny nodded.

'Would you consider holding a small vigil for Alex maybe at the cliffs where he trained? A lot of families do that. They spread the word amongst friends, ask one of Alex's friends to put the vigil on their social media pages, select a friend to say a few words and put some wreaths in the area.'

'We'd love to do that,' Jenny said, 'we'd been thinking about doing something similar. How does that help you?'

'It's amazing how many people will come up to you and tell you about Alex, their memories, how they enjoyed training with him, and some will just come to watch and observe.'

'And you'll be watching them,' Gary said, nodding his head with approval.

'Precisely.'

They were calmer when I left and had thrown themselves into the vigil planning before I got to their lift door. I was glad to be back in my car, music playing, thoughts spiralling. I was almost back at work when my phone rang; I answered hands-free – it was Melanie.

'I have some very interesting news for you from my gym workout this morning,' she said.

'Hi, Mel.'

'Can we meet?' she continued, talking fast.

'Sure, I'm heading into work.'

'Okay. The Grind on the corner in fifteen?' Melanie suggested.

'Then,' I said, and she was gone.

I got there before Mel and ordered my skinny cappuccino and a Piccolo Latte for Mel – a baby latte – because she liked to have a few coffees during the day and paced herself. I grabbed a table. She came in and dropped beside me, leaning over long enough to do some air-kissing.

'You look pretty chic,' Mel said.

'I had a client meeting,' I told her as if that explained the only reason I'd bother getting dressed.

Mel doesn't like to start a subject if she will be interrupted; it's performance art, but within seconds, our coffees arrived, and we were alone again. She looked around, lowered her voice, and began.

'Guess who was there this morning when I got to the gym? Trad Hassler!' she said, not waiting for me to guess.

'I was going to guess that!' I told her, disappointed I didn't get the chance. Mel ignored me.

'We arrived about the same time. Trad was about to take a class, and he looked hot, I have to add just for the record.'

'Noted on the record,' I said.

'And he asked me out!'

'Get out.'

'True story. I said that I thought he had a girlfriend, and he said it was over.'

'Is that so? But I only recently spoke with him; he referred to Casey as his girlfriend. Hmm, interesting. You can't go out with him, Mel, it's too dangerous.'

'I agree.'

'Oh, good.' She surprised me. I didn't expect to win that one so easily.

'But,' she continued, 'I didn't want to blow him off in case he was, you know, dangerous. So, I said I was having a hellish few weeks at work – tax time and all, and let's do that when I surface.'

'Brilliant thinking, Mel.' I sighed with relief. 'Because if you went out with him, Dom and I would have to do surveillance on your date.'

She laughed. 'What if we got amorous?'

'We'd be watching and taking notes,' I teased.

'Eww. Anyway, I've got more important news than that.' She sipped her coffee and continued. 'Kayla, you know, my CrossFit trainer?' Mel didn't wait for my answer. 'She pulled me aside after our session and said she saw me talking with Trad, and while it was none of her business, sister to sister, she wanted to warn me about Trad.'

'Really? I wasn't sure if they'd been on, off, or not at all.'

'Me either, but I don't think they've dated because she said Trad had just broken off with Kayla's best friend... who just happens to be Casey, and that Casey was a little scared of Trad.'

I had been watching Mel with the same concentration that I give to my soapies, and I egged her to go on.

'Kayla said Casey had wanted to call it off earlier, but Trad threatened her, so she was too scared to do so. He was dominant and demanding, and wait for it...'

'Uh-huh...'

'Extremely jealous. He told Casey he does the dumping, not her,' Mel said and sat back. 'Sounds more like ego than jealousy to me. But anyway, Kayla said Casey is relieved and doesn't care if she's been dumped. So I thanked Kayla profusely, and we had a sister sort of hug. It was good of her to share.'

'Hell yeah,' I agreed. 'I wish some of my boyfriends' ex-girlfriends had shared with me, especially that the guys were duds in bed.'

Mel laughed, 'think of the months of our lives we'd have back.' We chuckled at our private joke. Ah, such fun. But seriously, this was worrying.

'Mel, thank you. I think you've unearthed something very interesting.' I wondered if Alex and Casey were getting closer while training at the cliffs. Jenny – Alex's mum – mentioned that Alex had spoken of a friend named Casey. Hmm. Did Casey want it off with Trad to date Alex?

Mel opened her bag, grabbed her lipstick and reapplied it.

'I need to speak with Casey,' I said, 'if I can find out her surname and where she works.'

'Yeah, I sneakily tried that,' Mel said. 'I asked Kayla if Casey was safe... did she work somewhere where she had support.'

'You are good,' I teased Mel.

'Put it down to years of experience at sussing out guys and their exes.'

Given Mel's diverse dating life, I wasn't surprised.

'She works in government, the Fire and Emergency Services Department – in the communications team.'

'She's probably surrounded by firefighters,' I said, and we both stopped to appreciate that.

'I can come with you if you meet her at work,' Mel offered.

'But you've already done so much,' I teased.

'It's true,' she agreed and grinned. 'But I'm happy to keep giving.'

'Great, speaking of coming along, I've tickets to the choir's opening night – they're doing *Mahler: Symphony No.2*. Want to come?' I asked.

'No. I have my giving limits,' Melanie said, and with a quick air kiss and my thanks ringing in her ears, she was off, and I was heading to the office. It had been a good morning all round, I think.

# Chapter 18

I ENTERED THE OFFICE and laughed out loud when I saw Ed had put a large map on a board next to our Publicity and P.I. whiteboards. On the map were pins in different locations, with strings between each. A photo of T-Bear hung on the corner of the map. It looked like something from a crime TV program. He rose excited and rushed to show me.

'T-Bear is on the move,' he exclaimed.

'Wow'. I shook my head in disbelief.

Ed continued: 'He's been in three different states, and those are the confirmed sightings from Gabi's team after cross-checking the images and reports being shared on T-Bear's missing page.'

'Has a courier driver or pilot stolen him?'

Ed laughed, and then his eyes widened. 'Well, that's a thought.'

'You are brilliant; this is great,' I said, stepping back to admire his work.

'That's what Gabi said,' he added smugly. 'She's done over twenty interviews with local and national television, radio and newspaper, and their event line has been running hot.'

'I should charge her that publicity fee, but let's hope Grandma Ruby pays a bonus instead for bringing T-Bear home.'

'At least Gabi's a pro; she's been mentioning our agency in every interview she's done. We've already received a dozen requests for job quotes; we can deal with those next week,' Ed added, waving his hand like we didn't need business. You never know when it might dry up, so keeping good clients happy didn't hurt. Gabi was one of them who might become a regular client.

'Well done, Gabi,' I said, thinking about her with a satisfied smile. What a professional! I studied the map for a while longer. 'I can understand the cities, but there's a few obscure locations here, small towns... what is T-Bear doing there, I wonder.'

'Odd indeed,' Ed agreed, 'unless it is a road trip, but you'd think T-Bear would remain hidden in the car. But no, he's been sighted, allegedly.'

'What evidence do we have?' I asked.

'CCTV images, dash cams and phone shots,' Ed said, moving closer to the board, 'so these locations marked on the board are all legit.'

Ed's phone rang, and while he went to take the call, I sat down and got to work on my trains of thought, but a few were going off in different directions.

Firstly, were there any teddy or doll conferences going on around Australia at the moment where the bear-napper might want to show off T-Bear? Ten minutes later, that came up as a dud line of enquiry – there were a few exhibitions, but they were more about the craft of making dolls and teddies than buying, selling and showing off family heirlooms like T-Bear.

Next, were there any large buyer and seller antique fairs in the locations where T-Bear was currently holidaying? Maybe the bear-napper had hoped to get T-Bear priced and offload him, but with our viral campaign going berserk nationally, that's become too hard. I checked out the antique fairs and trader sites, and there had been two fairs recently, but they were not in the places T-Bear visited. The next event wasn't for another five weeks. Okay, no go on that lead.

Another thought struck me; it was a wild one, but it could have legs... were there any Australian Titanic passengers or survivors whose descendants might think they were more worthy recipients of T-Bear or had rights to him? They would have to know that Grandma Ruby owned a Titanic Mourning Bear, so they would need a connection with her or a family member.

I searched, and wow! Six Australians had been on board the Titanic among the 1300 plus passengers and 900 or so crew. I didn't see that coming. Like a dog burrowing for a bone – head down and into it – I barely heard Ed say he would get us our sandwiches from the deli down the road. My hand automatically raised in a wave of thanks.

I found the information – of the six Australians on board, three were crew, and three were passengers – next, the crew. I found Donald Campbell who hailed from Melbourne and was a clerk on board the Titanic; he handled provisions. I glanced at the board and confirmed that T-Bear had definitely visited Melbourne. I opened another site online and found that Donald had died at 2:20 am on 15 April 1912 when the Titanic went down, his body was never retrieved from the freezing waters. How many Campbell descendants were in the Melbourne area, I wondered?

The next crew member was Leonard White from Sydney, and yes, T-Bear had been to Sydney, too. I glanced at the red pin on the map marking his stay in the bustling city. Leonard was a saloon steward on the Titanic. A glance at the death list confirmed Leonard died, and his body never recovered either – so very sad. I wondered who was at home in 1912 waiting for his return.

Finally, the third Australian crew member was Alfred Nichols, also from Sydney, working as a boatswain on the

Titanic. I looked that up, and a boatswain was responsible for deck stuff, to put it technically – the anchor, the cables, the deck crew. A report said Alfred was seen opening the lower gangway doors to help get people above and onto lifeboats. A good guy. But after checking, I found Alfred, like Donald and Leonard, was lost in the icy waters.

It was so sad when you can imagine how excited those men probably were to secure jobs on the most glamorous and remarkable ship of its time on its maiden voyage from England to New York. If there were descendants in Sydney or Melbourne, T-Bear could have been there for that purpose.

The other three Australian passengers aboard the Titanic heralded from South Australia. I held my breath as I glanced at the map on the board, and sure enough, that's where T-Bear was now. He had gone from his home in Brisbane to Sydney, then Melbourne, and now he was seen in Adelaide, the capital of South Australia. My heart rate was up; I loved the chase. My phone rang, and I glanced at it impatiently – phew, it was Dom, not a client.

I answered quickly. 'Hi babe, everything okay?'

'Yeah, good. You sound busy?'

'I'm on a roll. See you at home for a walk this afternoon?'

'Yep, see you then.'

We said the love you stuff to each other, and I hung up, my eyes never leaving my laptop screen. So, the first guy from

South Australia actually came from Norway but settled in Adelaide. His name was Charles Dahl. I cross-checked, and he survived. He was in a lifeboat, but he went back to Norway eventually and died there. Hmm, interesting.

The next passenger was also from Adelaide – Arthur Gordon McCrae, an engineer. Arthur was a second-class passenger on the Titanic but could not get a seat on the lifeboat; they were given to the women and children first. He didn't make it.

The last passenger was a woman and a nurse by occupation, Evelyn Marsden, who came from a rural area near Adelaide called Dalkey. If T-Bear had been seen there, then the game was up! And, thank goodness Evelyn survived and helped row Lifeboat 16. I did some more digging and found Evelyn came home to Australia but, at the time of her death, was buried in Sydney.

I just needed to know now if there was any chance that someone saw T-Bear in Dalkey... I looked it up and it was about 90 kilometres from Adelaide or an hour and 20-minute drive. I got up and went to the board but there was no Dalkey on the map, which was not surprising. Ed had placed a few pins around Adelaide, so maybe it was nearby. Now, it was a waiting game until Ed got back.

Was T-Bear doing a tour for the descendants of Titanic survivors, and if so, why not ask Grandma Ruby for permission? It seemed like such a good cause, or was T-Bear's bear-napper not intending to bring T-Bear home?

Where was Ed when I needed him?

# Chapter 19

'DALKEY?' HE ASKED, HANDING me my sandwich. We both stood looking at the whiteboard. 'That's one I haven't heard. Where is it?'

My theory blew him away.

'This is the most exciting client we've had since—'

'Mona and the choir performed *Bruckner's Mass in E minor*?' I cut in, and he laughed.

'That was exactly what I was going to say!'

'I'm going to call Gabi on a conference call. Are you free now?' I asked, biting into my sandwich while Ed did the same.

'I'm free, let's do it. Her team might have a Dalkey sighting I'm yet to receive,' Ed said, and I dialled Gabi. After pleasantries, we got down to business. She grabbed her lunch while I told her my theory and my findings.

'That's amazing,' she said. 'I think you might be onto something there. T-Bear could have gone anywhere in Australia, but no, he's gone to the only place where descendants of survivors lived. Let me ask my team about Dalkey,' she said.

She was back before I could swallow another bite of my salad sandwich with cheese.

'Nope, nothing,' Gabi said.

'Still, that's not surprising,' I said, grabbing my notes. 'The population is about 10 people. I want to read you the names of the Australian crew and passengers that were on the Titanic, Gabi. It's a long shot, but tell me if you recognise any of the names... they might be family, a friend of your family, someone who has done business with your family.'

'I understand,' Gabi said, 'go ahead.'

I shuffled my notes and read out the surnames: 'Campbell – deceased, White – deceased, Nichols – deceased, Dahl – survived, McCrae – deceased, and a woman Evelyn Marsden who survived.'

There was a silence on the line.

'Gabi?'

'I'm here, sorry. You said Dahl, didn't you? How did that passenger spell his surname?'

'D-A-H-L,' I answered.

'My ex-boyfriend was a Dahl, Liam Dahl.'

After years in business, we were overnight successes – the hottest publicists and private eye in town with requests to do everything from raising an influencer's profile to finding a missing cat. So popular.

But right now, I was all about exes. I had to track down Liam Dahl… Gabi said he knew about T-Bear; they had spoken about it a few times. Plus, their relationship did not end well a year ago. So where was he now, and how might he have gotten his hands on T-Bear if he had? Plus, I needed to make an appointment to see Trad's ex-girlfriend Casey at the Fire and Emergency Department and find Lucy, Alex's estranged wife.

'I hate to say this,' I said, looking at Ed, 'but maybe we need an assistant.'

Ed groaned as he looked up from his laptop. 'I know. I thought the same thing, but we don't like people.'

'That's true, and we don't want to do job interviews, we'd have to meet a lot of them.'

'We could do word of mouth,' Ed suggested.

'We could. But then, if we didn't like someone and it was your cousin or Melanie's girlfriend, we'd feel obliged to be nice and keep them.' I pointed out the hole in that plan.

'You're right. We could get a temp, and then we could let them go if they didn't work out or hire them if they were great,' Ed said.

'Brilliant. Let's think about it later,' I agreed, and then we heard the lift door open, and we both groaned, hoping it wasn't a new client. What publicity firm said that ever? But timing was everything.

And then I felt an immense wave of relief – Jason, Officer Abingdon, walked in.

'Oh my God, I am so pleased to see you,' I gushed, and he grinned.

'Me too,' Ed said and returned to his typing.

'Really, well thanks,' Jason said, looking pleased with himself. Then he frowned. 'Why? What's happened?'

'I need to download with someone who knows the law and the criminal mind and just gets it.'

'Ah, yeah, you get days like that,' he said. 'Sure, love to. Especially since it is work-related, I can justify being here.'

I knew he would understand.

'I'll need tea or coffee, though, and biscuits. Maybe those shortbread biscuits of Ed's? They're the best.'

Ed smiled. 'Can do, Officer. Just remember my willingness to help the law, in case I ever break it. Those green prison outfits will make my skin look sallow.' He pulled the tin from his bottom draw and passed it over.

And then Jason dropped a bombshell. 'Speaking of prison, that's what I dropped by to tell you – Lucy's got a record.'

# Chapter 20

STEP BACK WITH THE right foot, and sideways with the left foot.... I looked up at Dominic and he was clearly enjoying the experience.

'I can't believe you dragged me here on the pretence of needing protection,' he said, his eyes narrowed in suspicion.

I looked as innocent as I could muster while concentrating on my waltz steps.

'You said that you wanted to be on hand to help me with my cases, so this is a big help,' I told him as we joined Lucy's ballroom dancing class. 'Besides, if we came earlier, we'd be learning tap dancing, so be grateful I didn't inflict that on you!'

The classes were held in a small dance studio – a former scout hall – the sign out the front still said scouts, but inside, one side of the room was all windows, and the other was floor-to-ceiling mirrors with a dance bar running along the wall. Tonight's class was an adult waltz with the students aged 18 to 80. A couple about our age swanned past and were much more advanced than us; I looked on enviously. Lucy appeared at my side.

'They are preparing for their bridal waltz in a few months,' she said, beaming at them, and then she turned her attention back to us and looked up at Dominic, who towered above us.

'My, you are extremely handsome, aren't you?' she said, and I laughed at her frankness. We were all the same age, and she was Alex's legal wife after all, but just the way she said it seemed so motherly and sweet.

'He is that, isn't he?' I agreed, grinning at Dom, who looked slightly embarrassed.

'Thank you,' he said, 'but I think I might be the thorn between two roses.'

She touched his arm. 'Charming, too. Thank you, Dominic. Now raise this arm a little higher,' she told him, bumping his arm up. 'Jesse, lift your chin, that's it, waltz on,' she said with a wink and moved to an older couple behind us.

I watched Lucy as she did the rounds of her class – nine couples learning ballroom dancing. She was lovely. Any doubts I had about her dominating Alex and coercing him into a relationship – as Alex's parents implied – went out the window. She was a big girl but beautiful. Her smile lit the room like sunshine; I can imagine quiet, sweet Alex being drawn to her like the earth circling the sun and that she made him feel important. Young and old vied for Lucy's attention and praise, which she generously bestowed upon each couple.

'Right, ladies and gentlemen,' she announced, clapping her hands, 'it's time for the progressive waltz.'

Dominic gave me a panicked look.

'Try not to stand on the old girls' toes,' I said with a grin.

'You haven't heard the end of this yet,' Dom warned as I went under his arm and sashayed off to the next dance partner, trying not to laugh.

After we went around twice and I was back with Dominic again, Lucy called the class to an end.

'That was fun, wasn't it?' I ribbed him. 'I bet you'll be begging me to return next week.'

He lowered his head near my ear and whispered. 'Oh, we're going to dance,' he threatened me, 'but nothing like this.'

After Lucy saw her clients out, she turned to me and Dominic.

'How lovely to meet you both,' she said.

'And you too, Lucy. Thank you for letting us come along and chat with you now. That was such a fun class,' I said.

'We try,' she laughed. 'I have wanted to dance all my life but was not quite the professional mould and very much made fun of in my younger years as a dancer of big build. But once I was qualified to teach, I set out to change that. Dancing should be for anyone who wants to move.' She pointed to a bench seat in the corner, and we sat down. 'Do you dance?'

'Like no one is watching most of the time,' I told her, and she laughed.

'I try to avoid it,' Dominic confessed, and she encouraged him.

'For a tall man, you were very graceful.'

He thanked her and excused himself to get a glass of water, leaving us to talk. I cleared my throat. 'I hope you will allow me to say how very sorry I am for all you have been through, the separation, losing Alex.'

She nodded and swallowed. 'Thank you. We were very happy once. And you work for his parents?'

'Yes, they have hired me on a short-term contract. I went to school with Alex.'

'Did you?' her eyes widened.

'I suspect it is why his parents hired me, hoping I'd better understand him, not because of my gun P.I. skills... I think Gary feels I'm too young for the job.'

She pressed her lips together and nodded as if a bad thought or word never left her mouth.

'Yes, he has strong opinions,' she said. 'So, were you friendly with Alex at school.'

'Not really. He was quiet, and I was nerdy; our paths rarely crossed,' I said. 'But he was kind, you know that, of course.'

'He was,' she agreed and looked out at the window as we spoke; it was dark, and we could see the lights of the street and our reflections in the glass. 'I barely knew him in the end. You know about *Lose it!*?'

'Yes. His parents said the company encouraged him to lose weight, and one of his colleagues mentioned the program, so he entered. They said that was the beginning of the end for you both?' I asked, not wanting to put words in her mouth, but I wanted to lead her to the reasons for their tension. I couldn't imagine her coming to his work and putting on a scene. She seemed so sweet.

'In a way, that is correct,' Lucy explained. 'He loved flying. His passion and the fear of losing his job was a motivator. It was perfectly safe for him to fly, but there was new management, and we suspected the airline had an image they wanted to uphold; Alex didn't fit that.'

I nodded my understanding but didn't interrupt. Lucy continued.

'When he decided to go on the television show, he asked if I wanted to do it, too. I didn't want to do anything that public, but I was happy to share the same diet; it would be easier for us both.' She sighed. 'Before *Lose it!* we enjoyed our lives. We worked hard, had good friends, danced, and the couch, streaming, and fridge were our happy places.' She gave me a grin, and I laughed.

'I've shared many happy moments with my fridge, too,' I assured her.

She became serious. 'Alex is only human… once he got a profile and started to lose weight, he didn't love me less, I really believe that, but women were just throwing themselves at him. Beautiful women that Alex would never have had a glance from before the weight loss were contacting him via his social media profile and the show is not even aired yet!'

'The temptation was too much for Alex?' I asked.

'Yes. He had several affairs, and one girl claimed to be pregnant. It turned out not to be true,' she added quickly as if saving me from chasing up that avenue, 'but it was relentless. I was broken-hearted.'

'But you must have stayed friends? I heard you were at the filming with him the day of his death?'

Lucy agreed. 'We had separated, but he was struggling. I think the novelty had worn off, and the push-and-pull on him was enormous. Alex was an introvert and not cut out for the limelight. He wanted to come home.'

'Were you happy to have him back?'

'I desperately wanted him back, but I didn't know how we could move forward. The betrayals, and I'll be honest, for a while there when he was sleeping around, he had become quite narky.'

I must have looked confused because she explained.

'You know, snide comments, jeers, ignoring my calls. I just wanted to know if we were on or off.' She pulled a tissue from her sleeve and dabbed her eyes. 'On one occasion, his work had him away for four days, and he didn't call or return my calls. I was frantic. So, when he wanted to reconcile, I had been through a lot of pain, and I had to be sure it was for the long haul and not just long enough to get him back on his feet.'

'But you never got that chance?' I asked and added: 'Were you with him when he came down the stairs that day in the studio?'

'No. I was running late. I arrived after the fall. I was with him in the ambulance and held his hand.'

'Did he say anything to you that might explain what happened?'

She shook his head. 'He was barely conscious, a few moments only. He looked at me and tried to say something but... nothing. That was our last time together. I don't know if we would have made it; it doesn't matter now.'

I exhaled, and we both sat in silence for a short time. Then we spoke briefly about all things including dancing, and I broached the subject of her criminal record. Lucy looked embarrassed, which is better than looking angry at me.

'I regret it now, but at the time... I was charged with assault, but it was an accident.' She sighed and told me the whole story. 'I was a greenie at University, I still am, but I've tempered my reactions. Along with several of my student friends, we thought we'd do a nude march to protest about a row of Jacaranda trees being cut down so the freeway could be extended.'

I smiled. 'Yeah, that beats anything I did at Uni.'

She laughed. 'I didn't really have a great figure for nude modelling, but none of us did really. We were rounded up and charged, but it got violent. One of the police grabbed a girl where he shouldn't have, and her boyfriend reacted. We all got a bit passionate. I took a few hits and gave a few back,' she shrugged. 'I was charged with assault, but I was assaulted too.'

I believed her, but she added: 'I have never hit or hurt anyone else in my whole life, and I can assure you, Alex was a big man when we were together, he wasn't harmed or threatened by me.'

I thanked her, and Dom and I waited while she locked up. Then, we all walked together to the dark carpark. I couldn't imagine for a moment that Lucy would kill Alex. Still, I must check if she benefitted from a life insurance or a payout from the *Lose it!* team given it was technically a workplace accident.

It was so sad, and I felt very heavy of heart when I left. Thank goodness I had Dominic with me. Maybe practising our dance steps might cheer me up.

*Chapter 21*

LIAM DAHL – GABI'S ex-boyfriend and chief bear kidnapper suspect – was a landscaper and owned a business – *The Green Scene*. Hmm, cute. His website was very good, and his projects looked impressive, but how well was Liam travelling financially? I checked out his website's photo gallery and saw that he drove an impressive Ute with his logo painted on the side. Was that his only car, or did he have a small fleet... just trying to work out how many places he could be in at once. He had a couple of staff as well. Liam's bio was a glossy affair, highlighting his good looks more than his talent. But if you believed his profile, he seemed to do well, particularly amongst the bored housewives of this town.

I whipped on to an ancestry site and searched for Charles Dahl and his descendants. His family tree stopped in Norway, nothing here in Australia at all. Maybe Liam was not related, but the shared surname inspired his idea and his chance to pass T-Bear off as his legitimate bear. I checked out his social media pages, not expecting for a moment to see his photos, but he had it public, not private. A quick study showed me why – it was more for his business than personal, and I suspected he wanted to be a landscaping influencer. There were shots of Liam with his shirt off gardening, shots of him digging with his shirt off, and oh, what a surprise, shots of Liam surveying his work with his shirt off. I hope he wore sunblock.

Then, I saw what I needed to see. I shot out of my chair. Wow, yes, there were shots from interstate at the same time that T-Bear was missing! I paced around for a few minutes, letting that sink in. Ed glanced at me but knew better to ask when he saw I had my narrowed eyes – locked jaw – pacing in a line thing going on. We all had our quirks. I sat down again. Back to Liam's social media pages and crosschecking the images, dates and times. Mind you, T-Bear didn't appear in any of them, which was hardly surprising, but there was no doubt from his social feed that Liam was interstate. I needed more than that – evidence. Evidence that he had T-Bear with him and a clue how he got his hands on T-Bear. His phone camera would be a huge find – those photos of T-Bear had to be somewhere, but my chances of getting that were slim.

I searched through the photos of him interstate and found what I was looking for – a few shots with a car in the frame, but he hadn't taken his Ute. He was in a red car that looked like a sedan.

'Can you remember any cars that witnesses have seen with T-Bear?' I asked Ed.

'Sure.' He tapped away, opening another screen and rattled off three cars, their colours and, in one case, a registration number – black, white and a red car, all sedans. Excellent.

'Got something?' he asked.

'Yep, ready to tell all! Can you grab Gabi for a conference call?' I asked, still researching.

'I'm on it,' Ed said. In minutes, Gabi appeared on our monitors.

I gave it to Ed and Gabi straight. 'I believe Liam might be our man, and I know where Liam and T-Bear are heading next.'

'O-M-G. Where?' Gabi asked, excited.

'Wagga Wagga.'

There was a momentary silence, as expected.

'Really? Why? What's in Wagga Wagga? There's no water in Wagga Wagga, is there?' she sat back, looking perplexed.

I grinned. 'No, but the *Relics of Titanic Exhibition* is about to open in Wagga Wagga.'

'Get out of here!' Ed exclaimed.

'True story, it opens to the public later this week. I've been tracking Liam's route, and he's on his way home. I rang his business pretending to be a client and they said he would be back later this week,' I explained.

'Clever.' Gabi applauded.

I grinned and kept going. 'The highway Liam is on now goes very close to the city of Wagga Wagga. He's in a red car, and we have sightings of T-Bear in a red car.'

'Brilliant!' she said. 'It has to be him, both of them!' she said. 'I bet he tries to sell T-Bear there.'

'He may or at least make contacts to do that later when the media campaign has died down. So, I have a plan.'

I glanced at Ed and noted his raised eyebrow expression. Gabi chuckled.

'Give it to us,' she said.

'I am taking a road trip to find Liam and bring T-Bear home. Liam Dahl is not the only one who can bear-nap.'

# Chapter 22

After our online meeting, I dashed out of the office to visit a lip-reader. I had two days to wrap up Alex's case before Alex's father considered going elsewhere. There was nothing like pressure to bring out your best. I wanted to see if a lip reader could tell me what Trad and Alex were saying to each other before they swapped phone numbers. It might be nothing, but I was desperate.

No appointment was necessary, so I ventured into *Hearing Link* like a girl on a mission.

'We can help you with that for sure,' a gorgeous, stylish young guy told me at reception. 'One moment, please.'

'Thanks,' I said and breathed out. I hadn't realised until then that I had been holding my breath in anticipation. Luckily, I hadn't fallen over and died... prone to exaggeration? He returned moments later with a mature-aged, thin lady wearing a very sedate, grey dress buttoned to the neck like you might wear if you did not want to attract attention from the opposite sex. I wouldn't have blinked if she told me her name was Sister Mary Theresa. But no.

'Jesse, this is Mrs Sonia Wilde. She can help you,' he said, introducing us.

'Mrs Wilde, thank you for your time,' I said, but I was thinking *no* – what an unfortunate surname for a woman who was clearly conservative and anything but wild. I bet she had heard that all her life.

'Jesse, my pleasure. Please come this way,' she said, and I noticed her voice was slightly different. I followed her down the hallway, and I was going to make small talk, but she stopped at a room and welcomed me with a sweep of her hand. It contained a few monitors, a lot of sound gear – headphones and microphones – and two tables and chairs.

'Please sit,' she said, inviting me to sit opposite her. The screen and the audio gear were to our left. She waited until I looked at her, and then Mrs Wilde said, 'Please call me Sonia. I am profoundly deaf, but I am a capable lip-reader.'

The shocked look on my face was unavoidable, and she smiled.

'I know, it often surprises people.'

I nodded. 'So, if I speak normally but articulate my words, you can easily read my lips?'

'Exactly,' she said.

'You are amazing,' I blurted out, hoping that wasn't condescending or rude. But no, Sonia flushed a little and thanked me.

Reaching for the USB, I made sure I didn't speak unless I was facing Sonia – she was used to silence; I wasn't, and it felt awkward. Articulating a quick brief of the situation that brought me to her, she nodded calmly at the end and didn't look surprised.

She turned from me, put the USB into the computer, and then focussed while I nervously waited, hopeful of solving the case... you know, Trad might say: 'I'm going to kill you, Alex,' or Alex might say, 'See you in the studio on the stairs.' Okay, I'm dreaming.

Sonia played the small piece of reunion vision and made some notes, jotting down the lines of conversation. Some she missed, others she got in full. Then she watched it another two times, and so did I, but I got very little. She truly was amazing. Twenty minutes later, after removing the USB, Sonia gave it back to me and showed her notes to me.

'Let me know, Jesse, if you think something might not be right, but this is the clearest I could get,' she said.

'Thank you, Sonia, you got so much,' I said, glancing down the page. She read from the top, and I followed along, reading her notes:

Trad: "Wow, wouldn't have recognised you."

Alex: "I know. I found the gym. I wish I'd found it years ago."

Trad: "Yeah, right. Do you work out every day?"

Alex: "Yeah. Luckily, my girlfriend is into it as well; that helps."

Trad: "You got that right. I'm training for the Trans-triathlon, it's full-on."

Alex; "Get out, so is she. Casey's amazing; she's in with a real chance."

Trad: "Where do you train?"

Alex: "The cliff stairs and a few of the local hill climbs. You?"

Trad: "Tr—"

'I'm not sure what name he says,' Sonia said, then continued reading Trad's dialogue.

Trad: "...and I have a few different places we train. Hey, I'm keen on getting some work with the *Lose it!* team. Any chance of an intro, and could we grab a drink or something afterwards? Maybe this Friday?"

Alex: "Sure—"

'Again, I'm not sure what he says here,' Sonia said before going on.

Trad: "We should swap numbers."

Alex: "Yeah, great. I'll be in touch and let you know a time." [Phone number exchange].

Trad: "Anyway, better get back to it. See you Friday then."

Alex: "Sure, see you then." END.

Sonia looked up at me on reaching the end of her translation. 'Does that help you, Jesse?'

'Oh Sonia, more than you know, thank you very much,' I said, feeling a little emotional now that I discovered Trad knew about Alex and Casey's relationship; he knew she was Alex's girlfriend; he wanted to get on *Lose it!* and was happy to call Alex a friend now that it suited him, and it flattered Alex.

The last thing Trad would want was for anyone to know about Casey and Alex, probably why he wrapped up that chat so quickly, and Alex's death happened in the studio the Friday after our reunion. Trad wasn't on the sign-in list, but was he there? I needed to get this to Jason and now.

I profusely thanked Sonia, paid the bill at reception, and returned to the office. While I drove, I wrapped the case up in my head. My guess... I think Alex was murdered. I think it was a crime of passion, not ambition. Handsome, athletic, Trad Hasler could not bear to have Alex Bryson – class nerd – steal his girlfriend. Trad was the class jock, the coolest guy in school, in his own humble opinion. If it came out at the reunion that his girlfriend had dumped him for Alex, it would be a delicious irony even if Trad insisted he did the dumping.

Frankly, we'd all get over it in about ten minutes because we've got lives, and they don't centre around Trad Hasler, but his ego was probably too big to realise that. He was and still is a narcissist. The humiliation would be unbearable.

## *Chapter 23*

JASON PICKED ME UP to meet with Casey – Alex and Trad's girlfriend – and I told him everything on the way. I wasn't expecting to go in his police car; so cool. I wanted to push every button on the dash.

'I didn't know the public could travel in a police car unless you were under arrest,' I said.

'It's not encouraged,' Jason said, 'and if there were an emergency, I wouldn't be able to attend to it while you were in the car, or I'd have to leave you on the footpath.' He grinned.

'Well, that's no fun,' I said.

When we arrived, Casey wasn't as happy to see us as I was to see her; a police uniform has that effect on people. She ushered us into a small meeting room, glancing around nervously to see who was watching and assuming she was in trouble with the law.

'Thanks for seeing us, Casey,' I began. I can imagine she would look good beside Trad, and Alex for that matter. She had long brown hair streaked with blonde, worn high in a ponytail, and she was glamorously wiry, like someone who was preparing for a triathlon and could run out of the office at any moment. Her arms and legs were lean and muscly, and she wore a sleeveless black dress that perfectly showed them off.

'I thought Alex's death was an accident,' she said, cutting to the chase after we all sat.

'It appeared that way, but we like to tie up all the loose ends,' Jason said.

'And Alex's parents are keen to know for sure, of course,' I added, not wanting to cast aspersion on the police who declared it an accident.

'Understandable,' Casey said. Her voice shook, and she rose, pulled a few tissues from a box on a shelf in the meeting room, and sat back down. 'Sorry, I still can't believe it. My emotions strike randomly,' she said and sniffed. 'I liked him and thought I was falling in love with him.' She looked a little embarrassed saying the words out loud, cried some more, and blew her nose.

I had already discussed my strategy with Jason in his cool cop car on the way over, so I led from the front.

'I know that you and Alex were seeing each other, and that is why you wanted to call it off with Trad, but he scared you.' She reacted quickly, as expected.

'Oh my God, who told you?' Then she shook her head. 'It doesn't matter. Alex was so lovely and kind, he was a gentleman, and Trad was the complete opposite.'

'Did Alex know Trad was your boyfriend?' Jason asked.

'Alex knew I was seeing someone, but I told him I was calling it off. He didn't know who that someone was as far as I know. I never told him. I tried to leave Trad, but he got so enraged and told me he'd do the dumping. Lucky for me, he did.'

I studied Casey. 'This is important, so please tell me the truth as you remember it. Did Trad know that you were keen on someone else or were breaking it off with him because of someone else?'

'Yes. I didn't set out to tell him but when he was ranting on about *who-did-I-think-I-was* calling it off with him when every girl at the gym is keen on him, I told him not this one and that I had found someone else.'

'How did he react?' Jason asked.

'He stopped dead like it was unimaginable, and then he went quiet and was furious. He stormed off, and then the next day, he rang and dumped me.'

'Is there any way he could have known it was Alex, because you know they went to school together?' I asked. Someone barged in, apologised, and went elsewhere to find a spare meeting room.

Casey returned to the question. 'I never told Trad, and he didn't train with Alex and me. Or...' she thought for a moment.

I waited, biting my tongue, which Dom told me I did when I was anxious.

'No.' She shook her head with confidence.

'No, why?' I asked.

'Alex couldn't have told him because I never said Trad's name. I told Alex I'd been seeing a guy from my gym, and I was calling it off.' Her voice hitched again, and the tears flowed. I touched her arm sympathetically.

'I'm so sorry that you and Alex didn't get a chance to start together,' I said, and she smiled and thanked me.

'How often did you train together?' I asked.

'I did three nights a week with Alex at the cliff stairs – Monday, Wednesday and Thursday, and I do three days with girlfriends who have also entered. It's better to gauge yourself against your own sex. I have Sunday off.'

'Me too,' I joked to lighten the mood a little and then added, 'okay, I might have more than one day off, but I always walk my dog.'

'That's enough exercise for anyone!' she said and smiled. I liked that she wasn't a junkie. Casey was a sweet girl. From what I could tell already, she was too good for Trad and would be a perfect fit for the lovely Alex.

Jason asked: 'Did you ever film your training routines at the cliff stairs?'

She reached for her phone. 'Absolutely. I've edited some and put them on my training website. My gym also got some footage of me while training.'

She found the video and held it up for me to see. It was too close – all I could see was super fit and sexy Casey running up the stairs in a fitted pair of lycra pants and a crop top. I'm sure Jason appreciated the footage. I glanced at him, and he gave a brief nod. Well done, Officer Abingdon.

'Could I possibly get any footage you shot, unedited? It would be an enormous help, plus the footage your gym shot. I am trying to see the bigger picture... who might be in the background?' I explained.

'You're thinking that Trad might have been spying on me?' she asked, looking genuinely frightened. Her hands went to face. 'What if I've caused Alex's death?'

Jason calmed her. 'Unless you pushed him down the stairs at the studio, you did not cause his death, and you have nothing to feel upset about.'

She nodded, unconvinced but temporarily consoled.

'I'll put everything in a file and send you the link,' she promised.

Jason fired the last shot. 'From what you know of Trad, is he capable of hurting Alex or anyone?'

'Hell yeah,' Casey said and laughed a slightly hysterical laugh. 'He'd do anything to be top dog, and then he'd be truly insufferable.'

Jason drove me back to my office.

'She was pretty hot, wasn't she?' I teased him.

'Who? Casey?' he asked nonchalantly.

I laughed. 'Come on, I was turned on watching her run up those stairs with that hot body and tight gym gear, and I'm straight... you must have been beside yourself.'

'I'm a professional,' he said seriously, and for a moment, I thought I might have offended him, and then he grinned, and I hit his arm.

'Nice try.'

He laughed. 'Yeah, she's okay.'

'She's single,' I said.

'God no,' he answered, 'all that performance pressure. I'd have to have a body to match, and I'm too tired for that.'

'I hear you,' I said. 'Besides, apparently, being fit can be a killer.'

'Looking that way,' Jason agreed.

# Chapter 24

THERE WAS A CAT fight, apparently. But the day didn't start that way. In fact, Ed and I had a peaceful start. We were in the office, frantically busy but with coffee and cake on hand. Ed's partner, Simon, had been baking. My phone rang, breaking the silence, and it was the lovely Tara, flight attendant and hugger, getting back to me to say that she had discovered nothing of interest about Alex from her fellow hosties. Bummer. But it was nice of her to try. We chatted briefly on the phone, and then like she had done last time, she threw in a comment at the end, which held weight.

'Oh, there was one small thing, Jesse, probably nothing,' she said.

'I'm desperate. I'll take it,' I said and made her laugh.

'Two of the girls are trying to get into reality television,' she sighed as though the thought was wearisome. 'Everyone wants to be a star.'

'I hear you,' I said, thinking except for Ed and me, who don't want to be stars, but I didn't say that to Tara.

She continued. 'I didn't see it myself, but there was a bit of a catfight between the girls – Steffy and Molly.'

'Oh, and how was Alex involved?'

'Well, it sounds silly, but Alex promised to take them to the studio for filming, and then I don't know whether he changed his mind or if his wife came along, but for whatever reason, he cancelled on them. They blamed each other, and they came to blows.'

'Good grief,' I said.

'I know. Steffy and Molly pulled each other's hair, and they scratched each other, it was terrible and nasty. They got suspended from flying for a month each, which made Alex even more unpopular with the pair of them,' she said.

'What reality programs are they trying to get on?' I asked.

'Whatever program will take them. Steffy has auditioned for *Brides for Shy Guys* and *Date Island*, as well as some cooking show, I can't remember its name. Molly has done the same and was shortlisted for a match-up show called *Love Story.*'

'Tara, you're great. I'll subtly look into it. Thank you again,' I said, and she laughed with pleasure.

'It was nothing.'

I got the girls' surnames from her and wished her safe travels. I then spent the next few hours checking them out. Was anyone besides Alex's wife, Lucy, in the studio on that Friday when Alex died? I printed out a photo of Trad, Lucy, and fighting girls Molly and Steffy, and left Ed to carry on. I headed off to talk with the receptionist and security guard at the studios where *Lose it!* was being shot.

The TV studio receptionist looked at the photos and could have sworn they had all been in the studio. I grabbed my phone and showed her Dominic's picture, and she said he had been there too. He hadn't been; I knew then that she was a hopeless witness. But the security guy was much better value. He folded his arms across his chest and took a good hard look at each shot for me. While he checked out the photos, I looked around.

'Do those cameras work?' I asked, seeing the CCTV cameras above his desk and pointing at reception. 'Would you have recordings of who entered the studio?'

'No,' he said and lowered his voice. 'Confidentially, they are live feeds to our security room, so if anything threatening happens here, we can push a button under the counter, and the security team can see what is going on and respond. They don't record.'

'Damn,' I said, and he smiled.

'That guy has never been here,' he said, pointing to Dominic's photo. Thank goodness for that. He looked at

Lucy's shot. 'She's been here a few times. I'm pretty sure she went in the ambulance with your victim.'

'She did, thank you,' I said. 'I'm not testing you,' I assured him. 'Just checking they are all telling the truth – if they did or didn't come to the studio.'

'I understand,' he said. 'That guy was here, came in with your victim.' He pointed to Trad's photo. 'He was here at least once that I remember, but I couldn't tell you which day.'

I nodded my thanks, excellent! The security guard looked at Molly and Steffy's photos. 'Yep, definitely this one and not that one.' He looked again at Molly's shot. 'She's been up a few times, really nice girl.'

I bet she was.

'She signed in, I'm sure,' he said. 'I watched her doing so.'

I had already gone through the sign-in book before showing them both the photos, and neither lady had signed in at any time in the past six weeks.

He clicked his fingers. 'Lucy, that was her name,' he said.

*What the hell? Had Molly signed in using Alex's estranged wife's name?*

I narrowed my eyes. 'Really. Was she with Alex when she signed in?' I asked.

'No, just by herself if my memory serves me right,' he said.

'That's brilliant. Thank you so much, your powers of observation are fantastic,' I gushed. So Molly signed in as Lucy.

Why? Because Alex wouldn't bring her, and if anyone asked, she'd say she was his wife. Molly, you are now looking very suspicious, I thought with a smile as I returned to the car.

But my joy was short-lived. I tracked down Molly, called her, and she burst into tears and confessed everything, which amounted to nothing.

'I got into the studio using Lucy's name,' she confessed, 'but that was on my second visit. I used my name the first time and said I worked with Alex, but he forgot to add me to the guest list. I showed them my flight attendant pass to prove I worked for the same company as he did, and the receptionist let me in. I wouldn't have had to if Alex had stuck by his promise. He said he'd get me in.'

'Did you see the security guy that day?' I asked.

'No, just the receptionist, but I saw him the next time I signed in.'

'So why sign in as Lucy?' I asked.

'Alex saw me that first time and was cranky. I didn't care. I met some friendly people and made a few contacts. But I wanted to visit again,' she said, sounding a little remorseful. 'I used Lucy's name because the receptionist was on the phone and the security guy was looking over my shoulder. I didn't know if Alex had banned me. I know it sounds bad,' she said, 'but if you want to get ahead, sometimes you just have to be super pushy, know what I mean?' she asked.

'Sure,' I said, not convinced. 'Were you there on the Friday when Alex died?' I asked, cutting to the chase.

'No. I heard Lucy was there that day. I guess that was good for Alex. You won't tell my work, will you... please?' she begged.

I assured her I wouldn't. What would be the point? I thanked Molly for being candid and hung up. Aagh, the trials of the modern-day detective. Several hours lost on a wild-goose chase, and it sounded so promising. At least I could put that in my report to Alex's parents as another lead chased down. Trad and Molly could have both been in the studio on that Friday without signing in, but without footage, how could I prove they were on the stairwell and pushed Alex?

Later that afternoon, Ed headed off to see our film distributor client – she had a new children's film for the school holidays for us to publicise. It had local actors voicing the characters and some catchy music, apparently. It was about a penguin, that's all I know. We were on fire this month.

Sometimes, it was just great to be back in the office. I could never do one of those sales jobs where I was always on the road. My quota of people contact was well and truly reached. I had the place to myself. I left the windows opened because only

Spiderman could climb that high, and it was nice to have the afternoon Autumn air coming in. We had the best building in the world, and if I won the Lotto, I'd buy the building to ensure they didn't replace it with a contemporary concrete box. I heard the lift doors open, and a voice called loudly, 'Good night.'

I didn't call back because our architect neighbour most likely wouldn't hear me. It was a courtesy he did every afternoon when he left so we knew that the lift's arrival marked his departure and not guests arriving – I thanked him previously at our Christmas party. I made a mug of tea and sat at my desk to catch up on everything. For the next hour, I waded through messages and looked at a few requests for our services because they had become overwhelming since T-Bear's publicity campaign. I didn't know which messages Ed had responded to yet, so it was best not to answer randomly. That's my excuse for being lazy and not answering them and I'm sticking to it.

My phone rang, and I jumped out of my seat... it was so quiet in the office.

'Dom, you scared me half to death,' I answered.

'Home alone?'

'Work alone.'

'Ah, it's getting dark; better lock your door,' he said because Dom always looked out for me. I rose and noticed he was right;

night had crept up on me. I locked the door and, shivering, closed the windows too. I looked down on the street while we spoke.

'When are you leaving?' he asked.

'About another thirty or forty minutes. I'm playing catch-up and waiting for Officer Jason to drop some stuff in for me. I'll go if he's not here by the time I want to leave,' I said. 'And you?'

'Now, I'm on my way home. I'll take Atlas out for a walk if you like – we'll have some male bonding time – and you can meet us out on the walk if we're not home when you get here.'

'That would be brilliant, thank you,' I said. 'Hey, I've got an idea for a quick road trip I want to discuss with you.'

'Fantastic! Let's go,' he teased. I laughed.

'I could do with a break,' he added.

'I'll be working you... navigating. Details when I get home.' I hung up after promising to call him before I came to meet them so he could look out for me. He'd make a great personal bodyguard.

I worked for a little longer, only interrupted by the occasional car horn or shouting on the street below. The area had a lot of residential units, and my office was amongst the café and coffee strip that the locals frequented after hours. I could have played music to fill the noise, but I liked the quiet.

At 6.30pm I started packing up. There was no sign of Jason, so I'd message him when I got to the car park to say I'd left. Then I heard the lift coming up. The doors to the building locked at six, so it had to be a tenant with access. I listened; the lift didn't come to the third floor. The building was creepy after hours when everyone on my floor had gone home; knowing the stairwells locked except for exiting from the floors, was some comfort. I heard a stairwell door bang. Again, I waited, no footsteps. It must be someone leaving for the day.

I logged out, turned off the lights, and exited. A glance at my phone to make sure Jason hadn't messaged. Nope, which meant he was working late, too, or something had come up. I'm glad we're both keeping the country running. I did the 'girl' thing – kept my phone handy in case I had to pretend I was talking with someone if there was a shady character in the car park, and I got my keys out so I could stab someone in self-defence. Death by key... must be a book in that. Truth be known, if they were close enough to be stabbed by a car key, the odds were I was a goner anyway. Cheery thought on an empty floor.

Lock the office door, check it's locked – done. I headed to the stairwell. The lift was old and occasionally got stuck – usually when you were in a hurry – there was no way I risked that after hours. I pushed open the stairwell door and hurried to head down to the car park.

I didn't see him at first until I got a few steps down. Then, I felt a presence in the corner behind me. I screamed in fright.

He smiled. 'Hello Jesse, you work late.'

'You scared me half to death,' I said, getting my breath back. 'Were you coming to see me?'

'No. I was waiting for you,' Trad said.

I froze. The implication of what he was saying hit me. Trad laughed. He must have come in before six o'clock and waited all that time, or someone let him in as they were leaving.

'You should have let it go,' Trad said. 'The police said it was an accident. Casey kept her big mouth shut, and the wife had no idea. All you had to do was play the game. But no, Casey told me you visited her and had been to the studio and gym, too.'

'I'm talking with everyone... I visited your best mate, Trent, too,' I said, trying to sound like I had nothing. Why would Casey tell him we'd interviewed her unless he threatened her?

'But you came to see her with a cop. You got her footage from the cliffs. You saw the text messages between me and Alex.'

Ah, he thinks I've caught him in a lie that would snowball. I was in big trouble; was anyone else in the building? The only place to run was downstairs. My heart was thumping in my chest, and I knew the stairwells were locked – I couldn't even run onto the next level and scream for help… my only exit was two floors down, straight into the car park. But Trad would be faster. He was bigger and not wearing heels like me.

As if he read my thoughts, he said: 'Those heels are dangerous when you're rushing down the stairs, aren't they?' His smile was creepy, and I could only imagine what Casey had been going through during her relationship.

I cleared my throat.

'Is this your thing, Trad? Stair pusher? First Alex, then me? I have a police friend meeting me downstairs, so if you're going to do anything to me, you'll be stuck in this building all night. When my cop friend comes looking for me, you'll be a sitting duck.'

He studied me, then grinned again. 'Meeting a cop friend, that's one I haven't heard before.'

'I'm happy to introduce you,' I said, smiling. It was more of a grimace but the best I could do.

'Little Jesse Clarke, all grown up and playing detectives,' he said in a sing-song voice.

I knew I had no option but to get away. I couldn't ring anyone on my phone without him grabbing it from me, and I'd be lucky if my scream were heard. However, I'd give that a shot while I was running. It was try or die, and I would fight until my last breath – I wasn't leaving Atlas and Dom.

The plan formulated in my head – throw my handbag at him, throw my shoes off and leave them on the stairs in the hope he'd trip on them, and run as fast as I could to the car park – it was the only choice I had.

Maybe someone would hear me screaming on the way down the stairs; perhaps someone was in the car park. Maybe I could fight back if I didn't fall down two flights of stairs.

A door slammed. A distraction. That was all I needed.

I literally jumped out of my shoes as he caught on to my plan. I hit Trad hard with my handbag, let it go, and ran down the stairs, hoping he'd trip on my shoes. I screamed for help the whole way. My bag temporarily blocked his vision, and in my peripheral vision, I saw him stumble on one of my shoes. It was an expensive shoe, worth the money if it derailed him.

My bag flew by me as he discarded it, and I heard him curse as he jumped over my other shoe. He leapt over the edge of the rail to cut in lower on the staircase. I wouldn't make it to the garage.

My screams echoed around the stairwell; no one appeared from any of the floors, maybe no one was left in the building. I felt him right on me as he slammed down behind me, cursing and swearing. He caught me on the lowest floor, swinging me around and throwing me up against the wall. I stuck my key into him. It might have hurt him, but barely penetrated his shirt.

He grabbed me around the throat.

'Nice try.'

And then my phone rang. His jaw locked as he studied me and released the pressure on my throat.

'My cop friend,' I gasped, 'out the front waiting for me.'

We waited, and it stopped ringing. Trad smirked, grabbed me away from the wall, and turned to lean me over the banister rail. The drop wasn't that big, but big enough to do damage if pushed.

Then my phone rang again.

'Christ almighty,' he swore.

Gasping as he restricted my breathing with his grasp on my throat, I told him: 'He'll force the door if he can't reach me; he knows I'm here waiting for him.' I didn't know if that was true or not. For all I know, Jason might have packed it in for the night and that could be Mum calling.

He pulled me back away from the stair rail and shoved me against the wall again.

'Answer it and tell him you've left and you'll see him tomorrow. One false move, and you'll be dead before he can barge his way in here. Got it?'

I couldn't move my head enough to nod, and my voice was shaky. I reached into my coat pocket for my phone; thank God I'd pulled it out of my handbag earlier. It was Jason.

*Please be here!*

'Hi,' I answered.

'Hi Jess, sorry I'm late. I'm at your work but I'm guessing you're not.'

'I am,' I said.

Trad's grip tightened on me, his arm pushing me into the wall, his face inches from mine.

'Your lights are off,' Jason said, 'where are you?'

'In the stairwell, help,' I screamed, and Trad grabbed the phone, threw it down the stairs and hit me back against the wall so hard I saw stars. He dropped me and ran down the remaining few stairs. I heard the car park stairwell door open. He was in there. An exit door near the roller door opened out to the street.

I pulled myself up and staggered towards my phone.

'Jason?'

He was still on the line. 'Here, bashing in the front door,' he panted. 'I've called for back-up. Are you okay?'

'Trad's coming out of the garage.'

'He may come back for you. Go back up to your office and lock yourself in.'

'I can't. The stairwell only opens out, not in at night. I've got to go to the car park to get out. He can't get back in here, but he can get out through the garage door.'

'Good, then stay put; don't hang up,' he said, and I heard him take off, his breathing almost as fast as mine. In the distance was the wail of a siren.

I wandered back up the stairs, still running on some adrenaline high, sore and a little stunned from the hits against the wall. I collected my keys, leaned over to grab my bag and felt a wave of nauseousness. I grabbed it, straightened, waited until that passed, and then collected my shoes a little further up the stairs. I headed down slowly to wait outside the car park door, keeping the phone near my ear the entire time. I didn't want to risk putting it on speaker phone just in case Trad had fooled me and was still in the building somehow.

Jason's voice cut into my thoughts. 'Jesse, I've got Harrison – an officer – here with another constable. The garage side door has just opened; I think they've got him. But don't you go into the carpark yet,' he ordered me. 'Understand?'

'Yes.'

I could hear their muffled voices and what sounded like orders being yelled.

'Okay, we've got him,' Jason said. 'Can you open the large garage door with your remote without being in there?'

'I'll try. I'm on the car park level just inside the stairwell door; it might work.' Hitting the remote button, I waited.

'It's working,' Jason said. 'Okay, I've got eyes on him now; the boys have got him! I'm coming over to your stairwell door now. Don't open the door until I'm there just to be safe,' he ordered. I could hear his steps as he walked and talked. 'Trad might have come into the carpark earlier, and someone could be waiting in a car for him.'

'Okay, be careful,' I said, my hand on the door handle.

A few moments later, he said, 'Seems to be clear. I'm here, open the door.'

I did, and I rushed straight into his arms.

'It's okay, you're safe,' he said, holding me tight.

I couldn't let go. I'm alive. Maybe Dom was right, maybe this was just not worth the risk.

# Chapter 25

Jason wouldn't let me drive home and he wouldn't take me home.

'You need to go to the hospital for a check-up,' he said as I got into his police car.

'I'm okay,' I assured him.

'No, you're not.'

He was right, I wasn't. The adrenaline dump had gone. I was shivering, and my head and throat ached.

'Can we go to my local hospital, near home then?' I asked. I lived with my community all around me – work was two blocks from home, and a hospital campus was further up the hill.

'Sure,' Jason said, glancing at me as he drove there. 'Can you talk to me about what happened?'

I nodded and started: 'He surprised me.' I told Jason the story, stumbling a few times on remembering the details. My head was a little fuzzy.

'You're doing great; there's no pressure,' he assured me. I told him how I thought I had to make a break or face the music.

'Christ,' he swore under his breath. 'If I'd been a bit earlier—'

I cut him off. 'Jason, you saved me. If we hadn't organised to meet, if you hadn't come...' I put my head back, closed my eyes and let the nauseousness wash over me.

I know he wanted to hold me. He touched my arm a few times, but it was a fine line between comfort and overstepping.

I jolted forward, eyes wide open.

'It's okay,' Jason said and squeezed my arm.

I remembered where I was and why.

'How did he know to wait for you in the stairwell and that you wouldn't take the lift?' Jason asked.

I thought about it. 'The day he came to see me, I made a joke about using the stairs if he wanted to guarantee he'd get out. He probably took a gamble that I did. He'd hear the lift arriving from there anyway, so he'd have time to bolt downstairs and meet me in the carpark.'

Talking had taken it out of me. We arrived at the hospital entrance.

'You can just drop me here if you have things you need to do,' I said.

'I don't need to be anywhere but here,' Jason assured me. He parked in the loading zone bay because he could in a police car and escorted me in. I had to stop; nauseousness and dizziness were rising. Jason put his arm around me and helped me, taking all my weight. It was amazing how quickly you get seen when you've got a cop escorting you – I've sat in the public section of emergency for hours before with Dom when he's had an injury. I guess they probably worried that, being a female, I might have been assaulted or worse. I didn't know then that I had huge red welts around my neck and throat.

A nurse showed us straight into a small cubicle and closed the curtains. Jason gave her a quick overview that I'd been assaulted, and my head hit repeatedly against the wall. She helped me off with my jacket and shoes, and I lay on the bed.

'We're most likely going to keep you overnight for observation,' she said and put her hand up to stop me before I began my protest, and then bile started rising.

'I'm going to throw up,' I said, and the nurse had a tray in front of me before you could say vomit.

Jason held my hair back, God, mortifying, and handed me a small towel afterwards. I laid back and thanked them.

'Got private health cover?' he asked, and I nodded. 'Cards in my bag.' I reached for it and tried to get it, but handed it to Jason.

'I'll go check you in and ring Dominic.'

The nurse looked at him, surprised.

'We go way back,' he said as he found my purse and private health card.

'Thank you, Jason.'

'Sure.' He departed with the card, and the nurse put a warm cotton blanket over me and offered me some water. She told me the doctor would be along shortly, but that's all I remembered. I was so exhausted and groggy, and asleep.

The next thing I knew, a doctor shone a light in my eyes, and Dominic was pacing between the window and my bed. I must have dozed off then, too, because the next time I opened my eyes – it might have been ten minutes or several hours later for all I know – Dom was sitting in a chair in the corner, eyes closed. I studied him; he was quite beautiful. And I was super thirsty.

I raised myself to get a glass of water, and his eyes shot open.

'Jess,' he said, rising, and got the water for me.

'Hey, you shouldn't have stuck around,' I said.

That pissed him off.

'The woman I love is in hospital with bruise marks around her throat and concussion and was this close to being killed,' he said, holding his fingers apart, 'but yeah, I should be at home watching TV.'

My reactions were all over the shop, and I'd lost my bravado for the moment. I started to cry, and Dom went into freak-out mode… most guys can't handle tears. He held me and apologised profusely until I shooshed him.

'I'm sorry, Jess, but I can't do this. I can't wake up each day knowing this might happen to you. You're my life, I can't do it.'

I nodded, and that action hurt. 'I understand, I do. Can we talk about it when I come home?'

'Only if we do talk about it. It's killing me and you,' he said, anger rising in his voice again, and then Dom softened. 'But sure, not now.'

'I'm going to sleep now, and I'm perfectly fine. Can you go home to Atlas, or I'll worry about you both and him being home alone? Tomorrow, yeah?' I said, a little slurred.

'Okay. I'll pick you up here in the morning when they release you.' He kissed me, and I laid back down and closed my eyes. I didn't hear Dom leave, but I could guess what he was going through.

I had an overwhelming need to see Jason. A survivor symptom? His strength and support with no guilt attached? I'd keep that to myself.

# Chapter 26

Officer Jason Abingdon and his colleague, Harrison, sat opposite Trad in a good-sized interview room. I was outside, looking through one-way glass. Jason allowed me to watch unseen as I had gathered the evidence and brought it to a head, thanks to Sonia, my lip reader. Well, thanks to Casey, and to Mel for finding out about her and the list was endless. I'd be like an award winner if I started listing and thanking everyone involved. Jason had taken it further and spoken with the *Lose it!* staff and also got Trad's phone records. A GPS location signal placed Trad on site on that Friday.

I couldn't help but shudder on seeing Trad and thinking about what might have happened. Casey was right; now that I knew what he was capable of, he looked nastier – I wonder how I ever considered him good-looking.

'You've got nothing,' Trad said, smirking at Jason.

'Let me tell you what I've got,' Jason said.

'We expect assault charges, which may be upgraded to attempted murder. The judge will take an assault of a woman very seriously,' Jason said, and Trad blew up.

'Just hold up there, that's bullshit, I was just...' Trad stopped. Anything he said could associate and incriminate him in Alex's death.

'Just?' Jason asked, and Trad shut down. His bravado quickly crumbled. He might have been a bully and egotist, but his plans did not include being locked up and working out in the prison gym.

Jason subtly looked my way, not that he could see me through the glass. He wanted me to pursue assault charges. But Trad was going to spend a lot more time in prison for murder if found guilty – he'd probably get a slap on the wrist for threatening me.

Jason continued. 'On the other matter, we were led to believe that you didn't train at the cliff staircase and that other than the reunion, you had not set eyes on Alex since school.'

'Yeah, that's right,' Trad said, sitting back and folding his arms across his chest. 'Why would I talk with that loser?' He scoffed.

If the size of his arms and the fact he worked out intimidated the two police officers, it didn't show. Jason and Harrison studied him for a few moments, and then Jason continued. 'I have evidence you did, in fact, speak with Alex about getting together. You got his number to set that up and met him at the studio where he was filming the reality program.'

'That's crap too. Who told you that?' Trad said, leaning forward. 'Did Trent tell you that? It's bullshit.'

Jason delivered his lines with measured confidence. I would have been nervous sitting opposite Trad – he was wired and edgy. He hadn't asked for a solicitor yet, as they do in the TV shows, but I was waiting for it.

'I don't have any statement from anyone called Trent,' Jason said. 'I have footage recorded by Party People at your reunion; fortunately, you and Alex were filmed during your discussion.'

Trad's face fell. He licked his lower lip; I could almost hear his mind scrambling, thinking back on what he said to Alex and what Jason had on him. Then, Trad laughed.

'Okay, okay, let me get this straight,' he said, cocky as ever. 'Alex and I spoke at a school reunion for all of a few minutes, and you're telling me that above the noise and band music, you have something that will incriminate me for his murder.' He laughed again. 'Priceless.'

Jason smiled. 'Yes, that's exactly what I have. It shows you both setting up a day to go to the studio. I have your mobile phone GPS that places you in the studio at the time of Alex's death, and *Lose it!* staff members who recall you on set. Did you want a solicitor?'

Trad's mouth dropped open.

Over the next two hours, with a solicitor present for the last hour, Trad and Alex's phone and GPS records were tabled, proving that Trad had been at the cliffs and seen Alex and Casey together when he claimed he had never been there. They also indicated Trad had been at the studio at the same time as Alex. But we still didn't have any actual proof he killed Alex, that he pushed him to his death. All I had was a gut instinct that Trad would never let the class nerd upstage him in his love life and work life. The thought was just too much for him to handle.

Then I remembered Trent, Trad's best friend. If he was ever going to do the right thing, now was the time – if he knew anything, if Trad had boasted to him and I could have put money on the fact he would – now was the time to spill it. When Officer Jason stepped out of the interview room, I mentioned that to him, and he agreed. He sent another police officer to bring Trent in. I believe Trent's heart still had some good in it; let's hope that faith was justified.

I was back at work after midday the next day – no sick leave for me. Ed was being very wary around me until I shut that down.

'Ed, stop it!'

'What?' he said, looking around.

'It's me. Stop pussyfooting around me like I'm glass; I can't bear it,' I said, swivelling my chair to face him.

He rolled his eyes. 'Sorry, but you have all this bruising,' he said, waving over his throat area. 'And you look so sore and sorry, and I'd be very sorry if you were no longer here.'

I softened and smiled at him. 'Me too, but I'm okay, I promise.'

'How's Dom taking it?'

'He's cranky.'

'He couldn't rescue you.'

I nodded. 'Men,' we said in unison.

'Jason saved my life. Thank God he was coming here to collect the transcript from me or... you know.'

Ed nodded. 'I told you he liked you a little more than most. Anyone else would have told you to email it to them, but he wanted to drop in. Might have saved your life, bless the good officer.'

I nodded. Ed was right, but I couldn't talk about it yet.

'Does it put you off doing it, you know the job?' Ed asked.

'No. Not every case will turn out like this.'

Ed sat back and webbed his fingers over his chest.

'What?' I asked him, narrowing my eyes.

'Well, there was the time Dom got bashed up.'

I nodded. 'I know. Maybe I should give it up or at least be more selective about my cases. I don't know,' I sighed and shrugged, 'but at the moment, it's like a huge elephant sitting in the room with Dom and me, and we're both pretending it's not there.'

And then Jason arrived, and we headed off to do a satisfying and unpleasant job.

I've only had one prior case where a parent had lost a child, and it differed from this situation. So, I didn't know how Alex's parents – Gary and Jenny – would react when I met them late that afternoon to update them about Trad and wrap up my involvement.

'We have a suspect in Alex's death, but we're not completely in the clear,' I said, sitting with Officer Jason Abingdon on the couch in their living room.

Jenny gasped, and Gary's hand went straight to his throat as if he couldn't breathe.

Jason told them everything, and I let him. I wanted it to come from him because it was credible and believable when delivered by a person in uniform. Besides, it was painful for me – my throat was still raw from the choking. Jason was generous in pointing out my work got us to this point. Not to mention by the deadline Gary set.

Jason finished by saying: 'We have enough to consider him a suspect, but we will need more to bring a case against him, and unless we can place him on that staircase pushing Alex, it will be tough. But the police will re-open this investigation.'

'Yes!' Gary hissed as if his team had just scored a goal.

I spoke up to elaborate. 'Without a confession, we might not get a conviction yet – we have the accused in the location, we have a motive, we have the fact he similarly threatened Casey and me, and he did not deny it when I accused him of Alex's death...'

'I'm sorry about that,' Gary said, looking at my bruised throat.

I nodded my thanks and continued. 'But it's our word against his. It's fairly circumstantial,' I said with a look at Jason, and he nodded in agreement. I didn't mention we were still trying to get more out of Trad's best friend Trent, who agreed that Trad could be dangerous but swore black and blue that Trad did not share anything with him, like the fact he was going to kill Alex.

Jason added: 'Footage and witnesses are vital. But please, let it take its course now. We must do it right so the case doesn't get thrown out.'

Gary nodded. 'I understand.' He looked relieved. It was the easiest way for him to justify the loss of his son, rather than believing Alex slipped and fell – all those years of love, potential and hope just gone in a flash.

'Oh Jesse, thank you,' Jenny said between tears.

'He was a kind and gentle soul, one of the nicest boys at school,' I said. 'That's what Casey saw in him too... they were falling in love.'

'I want to meet her,' Jenny said.

'She told me she was coming to the vigil,' I said. 'Her gym had a poster on their noticeboard; you did a good job.'

'If she hadn't got involved with Alex, he'd still be alive,' Gary said, still seeking people to blame his son's death on.

'If we can prove it, there is only one person responsible for your son's death, Mr Bryson, and we have him in our sights now,' Jason reminded him. 'Let's hope we get justice, but if there is a trial, the process will be a drawn-out affair. Nothing moves too quickly through the courts these days, and we need more evidence.'

Gary nodded and looked at me. 'Thank you. You did a good job.'

Wow, high praise – big deal. I didn't like Gary nor sought his approval. But I wanted him to have closure. I wanted Jenny to have it more.

'The vigil Friday fortnight marks exactly one month since Alex's death. Will you come?' Jenny asked me.

We'd be back from our road trip by then. 'Of course,' I said, 'it would be my honour.'

# Chapter 27

MY AFTERNOON CONVERSATION WITH Ed went as expected – not great.

'I can't believe you're going on a work road trip without me?' he wailed.

Sitting on the edge of my desk, I crossed my arms and narrowed my eyes at him.

'You are not fooling me, Ed,' I said. 'You and Simon are not road trip guys... you're more winery and theatre guys. You would hate sitting in the car for endless hours, taking turns playing each other's music lists or podcasts, counting the hours until the next stop to break the monotony, and finding that "*I spy with my little eye*" doesn't work that well in the outback when the scenery can stay the same for hours on end.'

'Fine,' he grumbled. 'But it means I'll have to break in the temp on my own, or temps if they don't work out.'

'Ah yes, well, let's cancel that,' I suggested.

'God no, I have work to offload,' he said, coming clean.

Then I got it and grinned.

'Ah-ha! You don't want to go to the opening night for *Exotic Theatre,* and you were hoping to get out of it with the excuse of a road trip!'

'Me?' he said, looking completely innocent. 'I'd never do that to a client. Except them,' he admitted, and I laughed.

'You could slip out at the interval,' I said, sharing one of my old tricks. 'If you make sure you're seen before the play starts and at the interval, then just don't return when they ring that bell to take your seat after the interval, they'll never notice. Anyway, I promise that Dom, Atlas and I will only be on the road for a week at the most, and I'll be working and contactable the whole time.'

'Does Dom know it's not a holiday?' Ed asked.

'Sure, but he thinks he'll make it one, regardless. Rural landscapes, finding the best pie on the drive, spotting wild animals, and finding new and interesting places to annoy each other. Who doesn't love a road trip?'

I covered my throat bruising with a scarf before meeting Mel for a drink at our favourite cocktail bar. It made up for having to miss our weekly dinner.

'I am so glad you are not dead,' Melanie said. She was good at being direct.

'Me too.' We clinked our wine glasses in a toast to good health, and I took a sip before sitting back to relax and people-watch.

'Were you scared?' she asked.

I nodded. 'You know I've heard and read about your life flashing before you when in danger or threatened with death, and it did, seriously.'

'Was I in the flash?'

'Of course! It was weird because when I first saw Trad, I thought he was coming to see me in my office. That thought lasted about ten seconds, and then I realised he was waiting in a locked stairwell. Then he got this sinister grin thing going.'

Melanie grimaced. 'Creepy.'

'I know, it was.' I shuddered, and Mel reached for my hand.

'It's fine, I'm okay,' I said.

'I know you are,' she assured me.

I had trouble sleeping and was jumpy, but having Dom and Atlas in the house helped and going away to retrieve T-Bear would be a great distraction. Mel and I sipped our wines, and then I said: 'It's weird getting attacked by someone you know. You're initially not on alert like you would be with a stranger. There's this moment of disbelief and confusion...'

'Ugh, don't even think that. I don't want to go there in my head,' Mel said. 'How's Dominic coping?' she asked.

'He's quiet. We've agreed to talk about it when we are on the road, and we've both recovered – me from shock, Dom from frustration and anger, if that's possible.'

'That's not a bad idea... trapping him for the conversation.'

'Exactly, so we have to talk it out. No walking out or avoiding the subject.' I sighed, and Mel read me.

'What are you thinking?'

'That I don't know what to do,' I said. 'Maybe I should just give it up, Mel. It's not like I'm setting the world on fire.'

'Who is?' she snorted. 'It's about doing things we are good at, that add value, make us happy and satisfy us, and if our skills help others as well, that's even better.'

'Thanks, Mel,' I said. 'That's a good perspective.' My hand automatically went to my throat, where the bruising was starting to go yellow. Lovely.

'There are risks in every job... well, not accounting, I'll give you that. Not much risk, anyway,' she conceded. 'But doctors, paramedics, nurses, people working as carers, drivers, police, firefighters, teachers, you name it, there's an element of risk in all those jobs.'

'You're right,' I said. 'Maybe I could just take cases like T-Bear, not dead people's cases.'

Mel shook her head. 'That could still be dangerous. T-Bear's worth a lot of money, and if there's one thing I know from my work, it is that greed is not good despite what motivators say.

How many people have been injured or murdered because of money?'

'Hell yeah,' I agreed, then shrugged. 'I don't know,' I answered truthfully.

Mel laughed. 'Bet it is a lot. Jason would have a stat or two. Speaking of the spunky cop, what's his take on all this?'

I melted a little. 'He was amazing.'

Mel leaned forward and smiled. 'Do tell.'

'He just stepped up and saved me. He called in backup, told me not to move until he had eyes on me, cleared the area before he let me open the door, and virtually carried me into the emergency ward, which we got into straight away. Jason even helped me when I threw up. He just took charge,' I said.

'I love a man who takes charge.'

'Me too. Don't mention this to Dom,' I said, lowering my voice.

Mel held up her hands. 'When do I ever mention anything to Dom? This is a girls' night.'

'Yeah, sorry, no clause needed.' I chuckled. 'I appreciated Dom being there for me, but Jason didn't lecture me once. He didn't say I shouldn't be doing this or tell me to stop playing in his playground; he just stepped in and did what he did – keeping people safe. It was what I needed,' I said.

We both thought about that for a moment.

'Do you think he might act differently if he were your boyfriend?' Mel suggested.

'I don't know. What Jason does is so embedded in him, I don't think he'd ever ask me to change what I do when he faces that daily.'

'I have an idea,' Mel said. Her eyes were wide with the excitement of delivery.

'Go on,' I said, getting swept up in the possibility of a solution.

'You hire a personal bodyguard.'

I laughed, but Mel held up her hand to stop me. 'Hear me out, this has legs.'

'Okay, sure,' I said because she had got very serious, unlike Mel, especially after hours.

She continued: 'So you have a personal security person on call if there is any risk at all, or if you are working late or out at night... that person is on your books as a personal bodyguard, all the celebrities do it, and your clients pay for it – just work it into their bill. That should be do-able, yes?'

I thought about it for a moment and made the connection.

'Yes. Mel, that's so weird; you are channelling me! I was only recently joking with Dom that he would make a great personal bodyguard with his fitness and strength. I'm not sure how he'd go if he had to fight but he could call for backup.'

'It's a deterrent,' Mel said. 'A girl alone is more vulnerable to attack than a couple.'

'True. Dom could do a security course or something to get more qualified if he wanted to,' I said, thinking it through on the run. But Mel was right, the idea had legs. 'Mel, you are a genius.'

She smiled and shrugged. 'Yeah. I think you need a backup service as well, if Dom is unavailable – some other professionals. I could help you source that,' she added, and I laughed.

'You'd be the best person for the screening job.'

# Chapter 28

We got away early.

The general rule was that the windows went up as soon as our speed hit over 80km an hour. Sorry, Atlas! But really, it was so noisy otherwise, and random insects flew in at your face, yuk. I drove, Dominic navigated, and Atlas settled in to sleep until the first stop, about four hours away.

But Dom would have to do a lot more than just navigate; he was plotting Liam and T-Bear's movements and secretly loving it. We were getting fed intel by Ed and Gabi as information came in from the T-Bear social media pages, and Officer Jason threw us the odd bone here and there.

We cruised along, enjoying the landscape once we had left the city behind, pointing out cows and items of interest. Open spaces, fewer people and no traffic were just what I needed. We were at about the three-hour mark when Dom sighed.

'No reception again,' he said.

'It's a wonderful opportunity to look at the beautiful scenery then,' I suggested. 'Look, you two, there are some more cows.'

'Oh, hang on, it's back again,' Dom informed me.

I gave the cows a wave – they were the beautiful caramel type. I'd already made my joke about these cows being the ones that made caramel milkshakes on past road trips, so I couldn't resurrect that one again. Speaking of beautiful, the phone rang. It was Gabi.

'Can you talk?' she asked.

'Sure. You're on speaker phone, Dominic is navigating, and Atlas is asleep,' I said, introducing the team. They exchanged greetings.

'What have you got?' I asked.

'Okay, you were right,' she said, and I smiled. It didn't matter what I was right about. Who was tired of hearing that? Gabi continued: 'I have a relative who is still in touch with Liam – my cousin, Nadine. I can't believe she's stayed friends with him!'

'Maybe she just forgot to unfriend him,' I said, trying to help Nadine.

Gabi made a humph sort of sound, so I moved on. 'Tell me about Nadine.'

'Well,' Gabi said, collecting her thoughts, 'she's 25, seven years younger than me and Liam, she's a nurse, about my height, dark hair – dyed badly, and kind of pretty but homely.'

'Right,' I said, drawing a picture in my mind. 'How well do Nadine and Liam know each other?'

'Pretty well. I mean, Liam and I went out for a few years, and we're a social family. The two of them got on because they both loved sports and always talked about football. She groaned like that was the worst thing in the world.

'Are they seeing each other by any chance?' I asked, and Gabi laughed.

'No. Sorry, I don't mean to be nasty, but Liam is all about image, and Nadine can't fulfil that for him,' she laughed again. 'But he was always staring at her breasts, now that I think about it. She's got curves, I'll give her that.' She gave a slight shrug as though conceding that point to Nadine was fair enough. 'His type is small, thin, blonde, and someone who is able to introduce him in the right circles.'

She had just described herself.

'Did Nadine put up anything online about your family reunion for Grandma Ruby's birthday before the event happened, something that might have alerted Liam to it?' I asked, emphasising the '*before*' part.

'Let me just check,' Gabi said. 'I'm going through her feed. Wow, she posts a lot... wait up, here we go. There's one post of her modelling a dress, and she writes that she bought it for Grandma Ruby's party. Then there are a couple of photos from the actual day, which got over 100 likes—'

Care factor of none on that, but I kept that thought to myself while Gabi kept talking through her observations.

'Yes!' she said. 'There's a post here where she's got a photo of some beautiful blue and white china in a gift box with a big white bow, and she's written – "Happy days and a happy birthday reunion at my Granny's this Sunday, can't wait" – it's a photo of the present she bought Grandma Ruby. It was nice, very tasteful.'

'Goodo,' I said, unsure what to say. 'Can you tell me if Liam liked or commented on her posts?'

'Sure, hang on, I'm scrolling through the 105 likes and responses. Yep, the little creep, he liked it!'

'Excellent.'

'So, you think Nadine might have taken T-Bear from the party and given it to Liam?' Gabi asked.

'At this stage, I think that Liam knew there was a family gathering and that he might have learnt that information from Nadine. That's all we can surmise from that, so remember not a word to any of the family.'

'Trust me, my lips are sealed until that bear is back in Grandma Ruby's hands, and then I can't be responsible for my actions.'

I chuckled because she didn't say that with all seriousness – I hoped. We said our goodbyes. Dom disconnected the call, and then I glanced at him.

'What do you think?' I asked.

'I have a feeling that Liam's been romancing and manipulating poor Nadine to get exactly what he wants.'

We'd stopped for a break, walked around a local park and polished off a sandwich and coffee. Atlas had his cooked chicken breast – one I had prepared earlier like they do in all the good cooking shows. Soon, we were back on the road with just under three hours to go for the afternoon driving sprint. After the first hour, Jason called – it was a very social road trip so far.

'Hi Jess, Dom and Atlas,' he said, scoring brownie points from me for including my beloved furry kid. We both greeted him.

'Where are you?' he asked.

Dom, the navigator, told him in more detail than he probably wanted, but that would teach him for asking.

'What's happening?' I asked, finally getting back to making it all about me.

'I had a few minutes to spare, so I thought I'd check out your suspect – Liam Dahl. He has a clean record.'

I sighed. 'Thanks, Jason. Couldn't you have broken that to me gently?'

He laughed. 'Yeah, disappointing, I know. Many a time I've been in the same situation. The most he has is a few speeding fines – 70 in a 60 zone. Dangerous stuff!'

'Well, maybe he just cracked – got sick of working his butt off when some people have everything, and knowing that one bear might make all the difference, he strayed from good to evil,' I said.

'You should write crime books,' Dom said, and Jason laughed.

'It's a motive,' I said, and Jason agreed. 'Well, thanks anyway, I appreciate you doing that for me.'

'Sure,' Jason said. 'Keep me informed.'

We said our goodbyes and hung up, and then Dom's breath hitched.

'Fantastic,' he said and smiled.

'What?' I looked left and right. The scenery was beautiful but hadn't changed in the last hour. A glance behind, nope, pretty much the same.

Dom was flicking the screen on his phone. 'Ha, according to Liam's feed, he's just arrived in Albury!'

'Great,' I said, sharing his enthusiasm; I don't know why, geography was not my strongest subject. I never scored a blue triangle with those questions in *Trivial Pursuit*. Dom, recognising that my reaction was not enthusiastic enough, simplified it.

'Since he's coming from Melbourne, he can go the Newell Highway or the Hume Highway... Albury is the logical town on route to turn off before he gets to Wagga Wagga,' he said, 'and that is where he is now. He's on the right route for Wagga Wagga, like us.'

I whooped. 'He's got to be going to the Titanic Exhibition; I think we've got our guy,' I said.

'We're nearly a day behind Liam on our journey, but we'll both be there tomorrow, just at different times!'

'If he takes that route. Does he automatically go past there on the highway?' I asked.

'No, he has to choose to detour to Wagga Wagga, but he is heading that way.'

I nodded. 'Dilemma... if he doesn't go to Wagga Wagga, do we follow him whichever way he is going and assume he has T-Bear, or do we go to the museum with the Titanic Exhibition and see if any bears are visiting?'

Dom thought for a moment and then answered: 'That's your call, but let's make it after we see what photos he posts next and where he goes.'

The phone rang again, and it was Ed from the office. We were so popular.

'Ed, hi, are you coping without me?' I teased.

'Good afternoon, Jesse, Dom, Atlas,' he said in his usual Ed style. 'Given how little you are in the office these days, I barely noticed you weren't here, but—'

'But?' I asked, expecting a drama.

'Regardless, I'd rather you were here,' he added.

'I knew you'd miss me,' I teased.

'This morning, I had to do the coffee run myself,' he said and chuckled when I groaned. 'Want an update?'

'Absolutely.' I grabbed the steering wheel and braced as an enormous truck roared past on the other side of the road. The truckies were great; they were on a mission and moved along. The caravaners, however, were not so good to get stuck behind. Of course I'd think differently in the future when the three of us were driving along in our campervan one day. I digressed.

Dom pointed at some emus in the distance – weirdest looking birds ever – and I nodded, watching them and the road.

'So,' Ed continued, 'T-Bear first. Our national watchers have had a flurry of activity this afternoon.'

'Really!' I almost squealed. 'Dom's also discovered Liam's in Albury from the photos in his feed.'

'Well, that fits perfectly because there's a couple of oldies on the case, and they think that's where T-Bear is, too.'

'Get out of here,' Dom said, 'that's brilliant. They might need the reward money,' he added as an afterthought.

'Who are they?' I asked.

'Earl and Pearl.'

There was a stunned silence in the car, and then Dom got some words out.

'No, seriously?'

'As serious as it gets,' Ed said. 'The two of them are just classic. I love them. They've been in our top five chasers, and I desperately hope they get the reward money.'

'What's their story?' I asked and seeing a police car coming some distance away, I quickly checked my speed, even though it was in cruise control. They passed with a glance my way and total disinterest. A quick check of the rear-view mirror said they hadn't spun around to follow me, so I must be innocent today.

'They're bush poets, and they travel around the country from one event to the other, meeting people, catching up with friends and entering the competitions.'

'There are bush poetry festivals?' I asked, still catching up.

'Apparently so, all over the country. I checked it out. There's the *Dusty Swag* competition, the *Blackened Billy* event, and the *King of the Road Bush Poetry Festival*, to name but a few,' Ed said.

'These retirees know how to have fun,' Dom said.

'I've been practicing...,' Ed told us. '...a verse about a stolen bear on the road to who knows where.'

'You go, you,' I said, and Dom applauded. 'But back to Earl and Pearl. Have they abandoned the poetry to chase T-Bear, or are they doing both?' I asked.

'I think there's a poetry festival in their general direction; those events are all over the place. But Earl and Pearl are on the same wavelength as you, Jess. They aren't giving away too much because they want to win the reward, but they're following the red car, and they've just sent through a tip that the car is in Albury and the driver has booked into a hotel for the night.'

'Did they describe the driver?' I asked.

'Yes, and he fits Liam's description. If they've been following T-Bear and saw him in that car, then I think you might have your man.'

Dom and I exchanged a high-five; Atlas looked up and then went back to sleep. He was excited, too, I'm sure of it.

'Right, we won't be arriving in Wagga Wagga until tomorrow afternoon, according to our navigator,' I said to Ed with a glance at Dom.

Dom agreed and continued: 'Liam should arrive there in the morning, so as soon as you hear anything – like if the red car has arrived in Wagga Wagga and where Liam's staying – can you get onto us?'

'Done,' Ed agreed.

'We've got to meet Earl and Pearl,' Dom said. 'I hope they're performing somewhere nearby.'

Ed's phone reception broke up for a moment and then came back strong. 'They're the only ones reporting the red car, so surely that must earn them some kind of reward just for useful information.'

'I agree. So, how did the temp go, or can't you talk?' I asked.

Ed groaned. Say no more.

'I let her go home early and told the agency we don't need her tomorrow. They're sending someone else in the morning.'

'Poor... what was her name?' I asked.

'Una.'

'Oh, great name, like Charlie Chaplin's wife!'

'No, that was Oona,' Dom told me. He loved his classic movies, especially the classic comedians, so he'd know that.

'Oh, right. Sorry. What did Una do?' I asked.

'Not much,' Ed answered. 'She was good at answering the phone but yawned all her way through chasing up the media to see if they were coming to the *Exotic Theatre* preview. She thought the water campaign was so boring and asked if we had any exciting projects. She just wanted to work on the film client's file.'

I laughed. 'Ah, the glamorous world of publicity, and you hadn't even started her on the choir stuff.'

'Plus, she got the coffee order wrong,' Ed said.

'She's gone,' I agreed. You had to draw the line somewhere.

# Chapter 29

THE NEXT MORNING, WE were back on the road early. We hadn't expected to hear from the T-Bear network for a few hours yet.

'Wouldn't it be great to be like Earl and Pearl?' Dom said as we left the town and hit the open spaces.

'I wish our names rhymed,' I agreed. 'Perhaps you're meant to be with someone else, someone whose name is—' I frowned, thinking, 'maybe Thomasina... Tom and Dom.'

'Yeah, not likely,' Dominic smirked at me. 'Wouldn't it be fun just living day to day, going around the country doing what you love? I hope we get to do that one day.'

'We're like them now!'

'Except we have to go back to work next week,' Dom said and sighed. 'I don't want to be a trainer forever.'

I knew the elephant was still in the room, or in this case, the car – our unspoken thoughts on my work and future career. Amazingly, we all fit in.

'I know.' I braved the topic. 'My publicity days are better because I bookend them with the private investigator work. Perhaps we can go around the country solving mysteries,' I suggested.

'Not ones where you risk being killed,' he said, narrowing his eyes.

'No, especially not crimes like that. Maybe mysteries like who stole the tea cosy from the knitting group.'

Dom laughed. 'Now you're talking.'

'We didn't talk about my work while driving yesterday, like we said we would,' I said.

'I know. We were both relaxed. I just wanted to be happy in the moment.'

I nodded. 'I get that. Do you want to talk about this now?'

'Yes, and no. It's a big discussion.'

'I have an idea to flag with you,' I said. 'You might think it's ridiculous and rule it out straight away, and that's fine, but...'

'Flag away,' Dom said.

I waited until I overtook a caravan... they don't usually start this early in the morning. I glanced at Atlas, who was fine in the back, and then I hit Dom with Mel's idea.

'You would make a great personal security guard for women needing escorting or who work in dangerous or compromising roles. You could build a business around it and involve some of your trainer friends and some security professionals. I was thinking you could do a course and—'

He cut me off. 'That's not a bad idea.'

I nodded. 'You'd have to develop a security guard voice. Something deep and threatening. You could practice saying, "Stop right there, Ma'am and take your clothes off now" on me if you like.'

'You would be my number one client, of course,' he agreed and grinned.

'Of course, you're not allowed to say that to other female clients unless they are on fire!'

He laughed and shook his head at me. Dominic rested his hand on my leg and sighed.

'I love you, Jess. I wish I could give you up, then you wouldn't have to consider getting married or giving up your P.I. work, but I can't. I can't imagine being with anyone else, ever.'

I got teary because my emotions are like that at the moment.

'I love you, too,' I told him. 'But if I end up making you miserable or vice versa...'

He nodded. 'I'll think about Mel's suggestion.'

I swallowed my emotion and said, 'Mel suggested I put your fee on my client's bill if the case warranted security.'

'That's a good idea, and it would save Jason from having to be on call too,' he said. I knew his ulterior motives, and they weren't completely altruistic regarding Jason's workload. And then his phone beeped.

'Ah, the network has started,' he said, grabbing his mobile office equipment.

'Liam should be there by now or on his way,' I told Dom. 'I wonder why he didn't stay in Wagga Wagga last night if he was only ninety minutes from the town.'

'He might know someone in Albury or have been tired of driving. Maybe he was struggling to get accommodation there with the Titanic Exhibition opening in town,' Dom suggested.

'Maybe he had an interested buyer in Albury,' I added. 'Anything?'

'No, just Saxon checking in, no overnight update.'

We drove hard and fast for the first four hours and stopped around 11am for a break in delightful Parkes. That left us three hours to Wagga Wagga, where if the action was going to happen, it would.

We were back on the road twenty minutes later, and I felt the pressure. *Chill out*, I told myself. There was no point in being anxious about it.

'He's on the move,' Dom exclaimed, checking his phone updates. He exhaled with relief.

I released a breath as if I had been holding it for hours. 'How do you know?'

'He's put a photo of himself at the *Thanks for visiting Albury* sign.'

I grinned. 'Dead giveaway.'

And right on cue, the *'track and find T-Bear'* network checked in again. Gabi's number came up on the car's hands-free phone line.

'Hi Gabi, it's D-Day,' I said.

'I know,' she said, drawing out the words. 'I'm so nervous for you; I wish I were there.'

'What have you got?' I asked, moving the conversation along in case Ed or Jason called too.

'I checked out the family. No other family members have stayed in touch with Liam, so it is just my cousin, Nadine, and oh my God, she likes and comments on everything he puts up. I think she's in love.'

Dom nodded and gave me a raised eyebrow look.

'You could be right, Gabi,' I said. 'I don't know how manipulative Liam is, if at all, but he could have been using Nadine, or might she have willingly had some part in this? Have you spoken to her since the party?'

'No, but that's normal for us. We're not close.'

That didn't surprise me. I imagine Nadine wasn't sophisticated enough to be in Gabi's friendship circle.

Gabi continued: 'She's very sweet though, and has always been a good girl. I can't see her doing anything like this intentionally. She would hate to hurt Grandma Ruby.'

'Then maybe she lost her heart to Liam and thought there was no harm in helping him,' I suggested. 'Or maybe she just inadvertently tipped him off in her feed that there would be a crowd of people at your grandma's place for a party, and he took advantage of that. I guess we'll soon know.'

'I hope so,' she said.

'How soon will your team have an update on the T-Bear pages?' I asked.

'Sax is talking with your Ed now,' Gabi said. 'There are fewer reports during the week when people are at work. We get more hits on the weekend when they are keen to go hunting.'

Dom broke into the conversation. 'Have you had many fake sightings?'

'Yeah, a couple has painted some poor Teddy black and tried to pull it off.'

'People,' I said and sighed.

'Don't I know it,' Gabi agreed.

Just then, Ed's number came up as call waiting. We bid Gabi goodbye for now and told her we'd call back later. I answered Ed's call.

'Ed, tell us you have news?'

'Oh, I have news,' he said. Ed loved a drama. 'Earl and Pearl are right behind the red car allegedly driven by Liam, and he is entering Wagga Wagga now.'

'Yes,' I cheered and punched the air.

'I've got their number. Do you want to call them? It might be worth giving them a warning to be careful and not approach him.'

'Absolutely, thanks Ed, that's great.'

'Sending it through now, you should have it.'

My phone pinged.

'Call me if something exciting happens, or I'll call you if I have news,' Ed added.

'Sure, thanks, Ed. Hey, got your temp there?'

'Yes,' he said, and nothing else.

'Right then,' I said and laughed. He was so transparent. 'Talk soon, and thanks.' I hung up. Poor Ed.

'Let's call Earl and Pearl, yeah?' Dom said, getting the number on the screen.

'Let's do it,' I agreed, and as the number rang, Dom and I both waited to hear the voices of our best amateur sleuths. Then Pearl answered.

'You've got Earl and Pearl, and you're speaking with the girl,' Pearl said.

Of course, we expected nothing less from the rhyming pair.

# Chapter 30

After ten minutes with the rhyming couple – Earl and Pearl – Dom hung up, sat back and laughed.

'Got to love them,' he said.

'I know. Poor Earl didn't get a word in. Can you call Jason?' I asked.

'Right,' Dom said, looking for the number on the phone list. Any mention of Jason was getting a frosty reception from Dominic.

We got the engaged signal, and when the message bank came up, Dom indicated that I should speak.

'Hi, Officer Jason, we've got some info. Can you call us when you get the chance? Oh, it is Jesse and Dominic,' I said. I couldn't be more 'coupley' than that.

Dom cut the call.

'Do you want to talk about Jason?' I asked, a little too quietly. I didn't want to, but Jason was in my orbit and necessary for my work. Plus, I liked him, he was my friend.

Dom had females around him all day at the gym, and I had to trust that process, so he had to chill and do the same.

'Why?' he said, a little too snappily. 'Is there something I should know about Jason?'

I sighed. I was very tender at the moment, both physically and emotionally, and Dom's tension didn't help.

'You stiffen at the mention of his name. You know that absolutely nothing is going on between Jason and me, don't you?' I glanced in his direction before returning my attention to the road, which hadn't changed for about the last hour. It's amazing how long and straight one stretch of road can be. Meanwhile, Dominic said nothing. He was like a tower of sexy anger, measuring his words and glaring out the window. Then he turned to me.

'What annoys me is that he was there when you needed him. He saved you. I hate that you needed saving and that he doesn't discourage you from giving this up because it's dangerous. I do that because I love you and come out looking like the bad guy.'

Jason rang back just then, and we both took a breath, preparing ourselves to appear neutral.

I answered. 'Hi, Officer Abingdon, busy day in crime circles?'

'Always Jesse, but I know to prioritise your calls.'

'Too kind,' I said, and then Dom stepped up, and we filled Jason in on our discussion with Earl and Pearl.

'If or when Liam arrives, Earl and Pearl are going to follow him and let us know where he is staying,' Dom said. 'We've warned them not to get close, and if he bails them up or suspects anything, they are to tell him they had a car like his once and were just taking a trip down memory lane.'

'Good thinking,' Jason said. 'So, what time will you be there?'

'About two hours from now,' I said.

'I'd give a Citizen's Commendation to any of you that got a glimpse of that bear,' Jason said.

'That's an incentive,' I teased. 'So Jace, if we get there and meet up with Pearl and Earl and positively identify Liam, what next? He most likely has T-Bear on him.'

'I've given the local cops a heads-up,' Jason said. 'When you know it is Liam, and he is the bear-napper or acting shady, call me. The local boys can bring him in for questioning.'

'Can you search his car or where he's staying?' I asked, knowing the answer but hoping he could pull some strings.

'We can search the car if we think we have reasonable grounds to suspect that it may have been used in connection with a serious offence like it contains stolen goods or unlawfully obtained goods, but we'd have to get a warrant to search his hotel room.'

Dom added: 'Most hotels don't let you check in until after 2pm, so if we are lucky, he might arrive, lock the car up and go straight to the museum.'

'Fingers crossed,' I said and looked at the clock. I needed to get to Wagga Wagga ASAP – Gabi, Grandma Ruby, Ed and Sax on the tracking team, were all hoping for an outcome, and I felt like I was carrying it. Ideally, we had to get there before Liam checked into a hotel and took his luggage out of the car. We could do that if we had no interruptions – roadworks, slow caravans or breakdowns.

❧

I drove like I was being driven out of town but stayed within the speed limits. Maybe five or ten kilometres over at the absolute most, and hey, who doesn't do that on outback roads?

'We'll get there in time,' I assured Dom. 'There's no way I'm going any faster or risking our lives for a stuffed bear.'

Dom laughed. 'Yeah, well, when you put it like that. Hopefully, Liam will be there for a few days, and we can stalk him.'

We sat in silence for a few seconds, and then he said, 'You won't risk our lives to save a bear, but you'll risk your life to solve the murder of a guy you haven't seen since school.'

He exhaled. 'Sorry, it's going to take some adjustment for me to get used to your new work scenario. When I fell in love with you, you were a publicist.'

I bit my lower lip so I wouldn't snap back a retort. That wouldn't help either of us. Eventually, I spoke again in my calm voice.

'Did you love me or love me because I was a publicist?' I glanced his way and brought up the subject we were talking about before. 'I don't think you're the bad guy for not wanting me to be in danger, and I don't think Jason's the good guy for riding in on a white horse,' I said. I did, but that was something I had to deal with and work out.

'It was just lucky that I told him I was going to work until late, and he was coming by to pick up the translation I had organised.'

'Or else I'd be organising your funeral,' he said.

I breathed out again. This was not what I needed right now; I was still trying to get my head right.

And then Dom reached for my hand and said in a voice I didn't recognise: 'If anyone else harms a hair on your head, I swear I will kill them.'

I looked twice. *Who the hell was this, and where was Dom? Was I creating a monster?* He needed to run or workout, and the sooner the better. Maybe talking about it in the car wasn't so clever after all. And then Dom's phone pinged, and he grabbed it.

'Ah-ha, it's from Gabi's team – from Sax – he says Liam has arrived in Wagga Wagga. Hold up,' Dom said, grabbing the iPad to check another screen. He grinned. 'Yeah, Earl and Pearl have confirmed the red car has arrived in Wagga Wagga. We have our man, the car, the location, the motive and the place.'

'We just need to be there and sight the bear!' I agreed, and we smiled at each other. Disaster averted for now.

'Thank God he slept in or did whatever he was doing in Albury this morning so we could catch up to him.' Dom exhaled with relief.

We passed a sign with the distance to Wagga Wagga remaining, and I did the calculations. 'We'll be there in under ninety minutes.'

'Great,' Dom said, not taking his eyes off the screen. 'Pearl has sent me a message. They've parked next to the red car; she's sending me a sneaky photo of Liam.' He looked up at me. 'Her words, not mine.'

A moment later, I heard the ping of an incoming message, and Dom opened the screen.

'That's Liam, he's definitely the red car driver.'

He flashed the photo at me and I glanced at it quickly and back to the road. Not that there was anything in front of me, beside me, or behind me on the road anywhere in sight, but you never know… a kangaroo, emu, or spaceship might appear, or a big bump in the road.

'I'm confirming with Gabi now since she's the best person to identify him,' Dom said, sending her a message. 'I'll let Ed, Earl, and Pearl know once she identifies him,' he said, thinking as he worked. He was rather sexy when coordinating our 'agents', and I told him so, which made him grin.

Things were hotting up, and the clock was counting down.

# Chapter 31

DOMINIC LOOKED LIKE HE was running an office in the front seat of the car – maps, paperwork and spreadsheets, iPad, his and my phone – and he was good at organisation under pressure. I'd rarely seen that side of him. I guess running fitness classes and managing a classroom full of young kids while trying to excite them about nutrition and exercise had shaped him.

We passed another sign to Wagga Wagga, and Dom caught it in his peripheral vision.

'Straight ahead, driver,' he said and gave me a wink.

'Aye, aye, my captain.' I glanced back at Atlas, and he sensed a change in the air. That window would be down as soon as we hit the slower speeds coming into Wagga Wagga!

The phone rang, and Dom accepted it on speaker phone.

'Hello you two, it's Earl here,' a deep, mature tenor voice said. 'Giving you an update while the Mrs plays a spy.'

'Hi Earl,' we both answered.

'What's the latest?' Dom asked.

'Well, the subject has gone into one of the trendy cafes, and he's sitting and looking at a menu. The car's parked nearby in the street and locked up.'

'I hope he orders big and takes a while to eat,' I said, glancing at the dashboard clock.

'Pearl and I are going to wander up and down the street and check out the town while we subtly keep eyes on him.'

'Fantastic, thanks, Earl,' Dom said, 'is he still alone?'

'Roger that,' Earl said, getting into it. 'What's your ETA?'

I looked appropriately confused, and Dom answered: 'Our estimated arrival time is fifty minutes.'

'Okay,' Earl breathed out, 'well drive safely, kids.'

'Will do,' Dom said, 'and call us if he's on the move. We'll call you as soon as we hit town.'

We said our goodbyes, and I suggested that we ring Jason. Dom agreed, found his number, and hit dial.

'Bear update,' I said when he answered and made him laugh.

'Highlight of my dreary day, trust me. What's going down?' he joked.

Dom filled him in.

'Okay, this is what we need to do,' Jason said, taking charge from the police side of the fence. 'We need to catch him before he disposes of, or sells, the bear. It's easier for him to deny he had it when it's out of his possession. Given the trail you have on him, I know it is not hard to prove, but it would be great to eliminate the need to do all that paperwork and the risk of Liam getting off.'

'Hell yeah,' I agreed.

'What's best then?' Dom asked.

'Ideally, I'd like to get him in the car so we can remove him and search it, thus finding it in his possession. Or if we can get him in the act of removing T-Bear from the car, that will work too,' Jason said. 'I've got the local boys on alert, but I don't want to call them in with the amateur sleuths on-site... what're their names?'

'Earl and Pearl,' I told him.

'Yeah, right, or anyone else that might be hovering nearby stalking him for a reward that we don't know about yet,' Jason said, which was worth considering.

'No offence,' I started, 'but we don't want a police presence scaring Liam off either; we want him to do what he came there to do.'

'Yeah, I agree,' Jason said, 'and I've explained that already to the local team. Because of the valuables in the exhibition, there are a few extra cops rostered to keep eyes on the museum anyway, and they are in plain clothes.'

'Perfect,' I said and sighed with relief.

'How far away are you?'

'Forty minutes now,' Dom glanced at the dash clock. His phone buzzed with a message. 'Sax has got an update for us.'

'That's Gabi's assistant,' I told Jason.

Dom read out Sax's update: 'The Relics of Titanic Exhibition manager has a meeting at 3pm with Liam. Good job, Sax, getting that,' Dom said, tapping out a reply.

'Right, I'll get my guys to have a quiet word with the manager now. Any name there?' Jason asked.

'Yep, wait up,' Dom said, scrolling through the message. 'The manager is Phillip Gunsberg.' Dom spelled out the surname.

'Got it. Okay, call me with any updates or when you get there. Don't speed.'

'Yes sir,' I snapped to attention and heard Jason chuckling as we disconnected. The phone rang – Ed.

'Hi, are you there yet?' he asked, his voice rushing.

'Thirty-five minutes away,' Dom said. 'All okay?'

'Just checking to see if you saw Sax's message?'

'Just got it, thanks,' Dom said and shared Jason's plan.

Ed read my mind. 'Don't panic, Jess. Gabi assured me they had not spoken to the manager or given him a heads-up. Gabi just pretended to be Liam's assistant and rang to confirm the appointment, hoping there was one.'

'Brilliant. The manager might have called off the meeting if he thought it was stolen property. We'd better call Gabi and tell her our plan so she sits tight,' I said with a glance at Dom, and he nodded. 'Thanks, Ed, how's the temp going?'

'Gone.'

'No!'

'True.'

'Wrong coffee order again?' I asked.

'No. He was great with the coffee but couldn't cope with two things happening at once – the phone ringing and lunch arriving.'

'Won't survive a day in publicity,' I agreed, holding back my laughter. I had a funny feeling that the temp was probably fine, but Ed didn't want anyone in the office. 'Got to go, we'll get back to you.'

'Sure,' he said and hung up.

The phone rang, and it was Earl or Pearl.

'Darlings, it's me, Pearl,' she bellowed, and we both sat back in our seats and winced. I saw in the rear-view mirror that even Atlas's head shot up; he gave me a look like it was my fault for disturbing him. Dom rushed to turn the volume down.

'Tell me he's not on the move, Pearl, please; we're about 20 minutes away,' I said, holding my breath.

'Darling, he is on the move.'

'Crap!'

'He's just paying for his fancy coffee and whatever else he had, and now he's walking out.'

I gave Dom a panicked look. If Pearl was speaking that loudly anywhere near Liam, the whole of Wagga Wagga could hear her. I hit my ear and showed with my hand a yapping voice. He nodded.

'Pearl, can you do us a favour?' Dom asked. 'Can you subtly keep eyes on Liam because women are better at surveillance, and a man won't be as suspicious if a woman is nearby, and let Earl do the phone reporting?'

'Good thinking, Darling,' she said, taking the bait.

I breathed out again and gave Dom a grateful look. Earl came on the line and started talking straight away without pleasantries... I suspected he had a military background. He kept his voice low, and we reached for the volume again.

'Subject in sight, and at this stage, he's just doing some window shopping, he hasn't returned to the car.'

'Thanks, Earl,' I said. 'We know he's got a meeting in an hour with the museum manager, and the police want to catch him in the act there, so he might kill some time before then.'

'I think you're right, young lady,' Earl said. 'He's just gone into a music store. We'll loiter and call you when he returns to the car.'

'Perfect, thanks, Earl, we're almost there,' Dom said.

We hung up, and Dom called Gabi, who squealed at hearing the plan and update.

'Right, I'll make sure my team knows to give nothing away now. We'll stand down unless something comes in that might be helpful,' she said. 'I swear when I get that bear home, I'm sneaking a tracker somewhere on his fur!'

We signed off, and the 'Welcome to Wagga Wagga' signs came into view. My heart was racing. I wanted to be at the car when he returned, see the officers search him and the car, or follow him to his meeting as he carried T-Bear in his bag. I wasn't sure which option Jason's team would take, but I preferred the latter.

The speed limit dropped to 80 kilometres per hour, and Atlas stirred.

'Can we call Jason again?' I asked Dom, and he hit the number.

'Bear Patrol Squad, Officer Abingdon speaking,' he answered, and we all laughed.

'Hi Chief Bear, we're ten minutes away. Liam's on the move and is now in a music store,' I told Jason.

'Killing time,' Jason said, as I'd said earlier. 'My cop buddy has spoken with the exhibition manager, and he's confirmed the meeting with Liam Dahl to discuss a Titanic relic.'

'Can we nab him in the meeting room with T-Bear and the manager, or do you think the car scenario is better?' I asked.

'I think the meeting is the perfect place, and Phillip Gunsberg is happy to play along. Who's tracking Liam now? The oldies?'

'Yep,' Dominic confirmed, 'they're subtly following him, hopefully.'

Jason chuckled. 'ETA?'

I knew the answer to this one now. 'About eight minutes to the city centre.'

We'd dropped to 60 kilometres, and I opened the window for Atlas. I could see his lips and ears flapping happily in the breeze in my side mirror. I wish I could do that.

'Okay,' Jason continued, 'can I suggest you park as close as possible to the museum where the exhibition is being held, and the three of you wait outside it? There's parkland there, I believe. A couple with a dog will look innocuous. Jess, a plain-clothes cop named William Miller, will find you. He's a senior constable with a uniform backup on standby. I gave him your description, but Atlas will make it easier.'

'Roger that,' I said. 'Sorry, I picked that up from Earl of Earl and Pearl fame.'

'Here's been in the trenches, I'd say,' Jason replied. 'Dom, can we distract Earl and Pearl? Can you shout them tickets to go inside? Put it on the client's budget.'

'Yeah, consider it done,' Dom said. He pointed for me to turn left into the city centre while he grabbed for his iPad to find the Exhibition Building.

'Wow, this is a pretty place,' I said, forgetting myself and doing some momentary sightseeing.

'Incoming call from Earl and Pearl now on my phone,' Dom said.

'I'll wait and listen in,' Jason said, who was on my phone.

'Earl?' Dom answered using speaker phone. 'We've just got the police on the other line...'

'Roger that, I'll make it brief: he's now heading down the opposite side of the street and shops, about five minutes until he's back at his car.'

'Great. Confirming the plan now is for the police to snatch him at the museum in the act of selling the bear, not at the car.'

'Understood, intercept at the museum,' Earl confirmed.

Dom continued: 'We're here, but we're going straight to the museum and Titanic Exhibition. Can you subtly stay with him and let us know if he doesn't go straight to the museum?'

'Can do.'

Dom continued. 'If you get to the exhibition, don't hesitate to go in; we'll reimburse your entry fees.'

'No problem, we've got our senior cards for a discount. Over and out,' Earl said, ever practical.

I gave Dom the thumbs up. I loved Earl and Pearl.

'Jason?' Dom checked to see if he was still there.

'Here. I've just spoken with Senior Constable Miller – Will – while waiting. He's there now on the grounds – there's a water feature and rose garden, and he's around there.'

'I've just found it online – Museum of the Riverina, Baylis Street, turn right,' Dom told me. He was doing everything at once and so good at it.

'It's in our sights,' I said.

'Good luck, bring that bear home,' Jason said, and for my benefit added, 'Over and out.' He hung up.

'Let's do this,' Dom agreed.

We drove down the city street, and we scanned the street for a parking spot. Dom pointed to one, and I pulled into it. Now to find Senior Constable Will, Earl, Pearl, Liam, and most importantly, T-Bear.

It was shifting sands given the sightings were from enthusiastic amateur sleuths keen to solve a crime. Until now, one wild clue led to a hundred more sightings, so Sax had his work cut out filtering out the authentic leads, but this was it, crunch time, and there were two clear lines of enquiry: some sleuths had seen the red car with the bear in it, other sleuths had seen the man with T-bear taking the bear's photo. As far as we knew, Earl and Pearl were the only remaining sleuths on the money and had put the two together.

That was about to become unstuck.

# Chapter 32

It all happened so fast, and yet it felt like it was in slow motion. I know that sounds weird, but it was the best way to describe it. Banners were everywhere promoting the Relics of Titanic Exhibition, and it looked exciting! Just as Dominic, Atlas, and I found a parking spot and I turned the ignition off, the phone rang again.

'Earl?' Dom said. The men didn't mince words.

'He's returned to the car, got a small black suitcase out and is walking up the street towards the museum. We have eyes on him and are following.'

'Great. Thanks, Earl. We're about to head to the park near the museum. Jesse is meeting a plain-clothes police officer, and they'll follow Liam and head inside. Atlas and I will meet you and Pearl outside, act like we're relatives. But if you want to follow Liam in, that's fine. Just buy your tickets, and we'll fix you up later, as we discussed.'

'Roger that, we'll see how it plays out. Over and out,' Earl said and hung up.

We were here at last. We got out of the car, and I could barely walk for a moment from sitting for so long. Hooking on Atlas's lead, I locked up the car, and the three of us hurried over to the fountain area while trying to look casual and relaxed. Then I saw him from a distance – Liam walking with the black bag – it looked like a large camera case.

Nudging Dom, he looked in the direction and nodded.

'So weird seeing him at last,' I whispered to Dom. 'I feel like I'm on a set of a movie.'

He grinned. 'I know. Don't you love it when a plan comes together?'

'You were amazing. I could not have done this without you. You are so good under pressure.'

'It was fun,' he admitted, 'a good adrenaline rush.'

'Are you sure you don't want to go with the Senior Constable up to the meeting room and spring out to surprise Liam?' I asked, smiling up at Dom.

He shook his head. 'No, it's your case; you have the satisfaction of closing it. I was happy to be of service, so was Ed, I imagine... maybe there are some parallels,' he said, but that thought was quickly lost as Earl and Pearl came into sight. She gave us a subtle wave; Earl was poker-faced.

We stopped near the fountain, and Atlas enjoyed his freedom, sniffing the area. I heard a voice.

'Hi, Jesse.'

I turned, and a guy in his thirties said in a lower voice: 'Senior Constable William Miller.'

'Senior Constable,' I said, 'this is my partner, Dominic, and furry kid, Atlas.'

The men shook hands, and Atlas got a pat.

'Ready?' he asked me as we both subtly kept Liam in sight. 'Let's head upstairs. The manager will have the meeting in an area where we can hear what's going on so we can make the arrest as needed. I've got two officers nearby.'

'Great,' I said. I turned to Dom and handed over Atlas, leaving the boys to wander around and greet Earl and Pearl.

As Will and I walked away, loud shouting behind us rooted us to the spot. We turned as all hell broke loose.

Out of nowhere, a young hippy-looking couple began running towards Liam, who was now in our direct line of sight. The guy yelled out.

'Bear stealer, stop, this is a citizen arrest!'

Liam turned, his eyes wide with surprise, his mouth dropped open, and then he took off, running directly ahead, straight towards me!

Dom called my name to warn me, Pearl screamed as the hippy guy leapt at Liam, and Hippy's girlfriend ran behind, trying to film the whole thing on her phone. Senior Constable Will pushed me out of the way, but Atlas, sensing I was in danger, broke free from Dom and ran towards me.

The hippy guy knocked Liam to the ground, the black bag flew from Liam's arms and broke open when it hit the ground, T-Bear went flying. Atlas jumped on Liam, the hippy guy fell across Liam's legs. Officer Will reached up and caught T-Bear in full flight, and Pearl started hitting Liam with her handbag.

A policewoman rushed to Officer Will's side.

'Cuff the one on the ground,' Will ordered, and the young female officer raced to Liam. Earl pulled Pearl away, Dom grabbed Atlas, Will held custody of T-Bear, and the policewoman pulled a cuffed Liam to his feet. Hippy dude jumped up and cheered; his girlfriend embraced him. Meanwhile, Earl and Pearl stood by, their mouths open. I re-joined Dom and Atlas; T-Bear was saved.

The photo that would appear on the newspaper's front page tomorrow was priceless.

# Chapter 33

It truly was a happy hour when we all got together Friday week in the publicity office, and a full house – even Gabi came along to celebrate the closure of the case. Plus, our new temp, Deidre, joined in. Yes, Ed found one he could tolerate, even liked. Despite the avalanche of work and offers that Ed and I had pouring in, Dom, Atlas, and I continued on our road trip for the week. It was great and just what we needed.

Mel laughed when she saw the framed newspaper front page on the wall – a welcome home present from Ed.

'It's a great photo,' she said, looking from the newspaper to me and back, 'and a really good one of you, Jesse!'

'It's because I'm running towards Atlas and not posing for it,' I explained to Gabi, 'I'm not very photogenic. But from now on, I will get a running start in all my photos!' Gabi and Mel laughed, picturing me on the starting line.

'I think you take a great photo,' Dom said, earning himself an adoring smile. Love was blind, after all.

The newspaper headline read: *"Panda-monium: caught with their bear-hands!"* T-Bear was right in the centre of the shot, in Senior Constable Will Miller's arms. Atlas was standing on top of Liam, making a dog arrest, and sprawled across Liam's legs was the hippy guy. Dominic, Earl and Pearl all stood by, looking shocked. Liam was looking up and back with his mouth wide open like a stunned mullet. I was running towards Atlas and the policewoman was coming from the other direction. Hippy's girlfriend was only just in the shot as she filmed the scene.

'This is a better fare than you usually come up with,' Officer Jason said, helping himself to some cheese and biscuits.

'Deirdre,' Ed said and nodded to our new mature temp. She brushed off the compliment. 'Deidre is a lifesaver,' Ed continued. 'Our work requests have gone through the roof, the phone's been ringing like crazy, and Deidre has responded to everyone. She has put their request on a spreadsheet, eliminated those clients that we wouldn't take on and got our publicity reports to existing clients, and that was just her first day!'

'Oh, go on with you,' she joked, but Ed was right, we loved her – even after just two days with Deidre, I realised how good she was for us. She was like the Mary Poppins of office temps – mature, short grey hair, small, thin, dressed in a neat shirt and pants with sensible shoes, and sparkling blue eyes. Best of all, I discovered on my return that Deidre would say things like: 'You don't need to be doing that; give it to me.' The best sentence ever.

'You're indispensable; Ed and I are not so,' I said, and she laughed.

'So, tell us what happened *after* the front page,' Mel said, and everyone looked at me.

'Well, it was a team effort; everyone was involved.'

'It takes a village to solve a crime!' Jason said with a wise look formed from years of policing.

I continued. 'Liam confessed to kidnapping T-Bear and trying to sell him. He had it all worked out and would come out of it well ahead. Initially, Liam intended to send a ransom note, hence the false account and the photos of T-Bear dangling in the water...'

'As if T-Bear hasn't had enough water exposure to last him a lifetime,' Mel said.

'You know the bear wasn't on the Titanic. They made him after as a gift,' Ed reminded her.

'Maybe, but he's a mourning bear! The last thing he needs is to be near water,' Mel pointed out.

'True,' I agreed. It was often the best way to manage Mel's strange perspective. I continued. 'Then, when the T-Bear campaign kicked in, sending the ransom note was trickier because he couldn't take more photos without risking outing himself. But he had already lined up some interested buyers from relatives of descendants, hence the road trip. Because he had the same surname as a real Titanic survivor, he came across as a credible descendant who was the rightful owner of T-Bear.'

I looked to Jason, who added, 'We spoke with those potential buyers, and they didn't know T-Bear was stolen until they saw the media campaign. Liam had seen two buyers before the media kicked in, so they were unaware. The third person he met with asked him if T-Bear was the stolen bear, and he denied it, packed up, and left quickly.'

Dominic contributed: 'So then his last chance was to offload it to the manager and owner of the *Relics of Titanic Exhibition*. Liam told him he was a descendant and had an authentic certificate, or as we know now, a fake certificate.'

'Exactly.' I picked up the story. 'It turns out that he's not related to the Charles Dahl who survived the Titanic sinking and died in Norway eventually, but Liam is enterprising.'

Gabi snorted. 'He must have been so excited when he was researching the price of the bears and came across Charles Dahl's name.'

'For sure,' I said. 'But our intrepid public detectives brought him down, literally, before the meeting and rescued T-Bear.'

'How did he get the bear in the first place?' Simon asked.

Gabi rolled her eyes. 'My dopey cousin, Nadine, is in love with him and believed him when he asked her to sneak the bear out so he could get it cleaned and repaired as his birthday gift to Grandma Ruby.' She shrugged.

'Why didn't she speak up then?' Mel asked.

I answered that one. 'She thought someone had stolen it from Liam and didn't want to get him in trouble. She didn't realise Liam was the thief.'

'Do you believe her story?' Ed asked Gabi, who nodded.

'Nadine's impressionable, Liam is charming, and Grandma Ruby always had a soft spot for Liam – they got on really well, so Nadine wasn't completely stupid to believe the lies he spun. Anyway, T-Bear's now got a tracker in him,' Gabi said, looking satisfied. 'I can't tell you how good it was to see that little bear's face again, and Grandma Ruby cried tears of joy.'

'It's a great story,' Simon agreed, 'and I've seen you all over the media this week,' he said to Gabi.

'I know, everyone wants to do the bear-is-home-safely story. The campaign was such a brilliant idea. Thank you, Jesse and Ed. You've saved T-Bear and given my business a tremendous boost,' she said.

'Our pleasure. It hasn't hurt us either,' I told her.

'What about the reward? I hope Earl and Pearl got it,' Jason said. 'They were so good.'

'They were great,' Dom agreed.

*Look at that: Jason and Dominic agree on something. How nice!*

Dom told the group: 'We had dinner with them at our accommodation that night. They're a funny pair. They are off now to the next poetry festival.'

I accepted a small top-up of wine in my glass and told everyone: 'Their information really helped us. It's great the hippy pair made the citizen arrest, but Earl and Pearl confirmed we were on target.'

Gabi agreed. 'Sax said the same thing, and Grandma Ruby laughed so much hearing about Earl and Pearl and the hippies. She initially offered a reward of $10,000: $6000 for whoever provided information that led to bringing T-Bear home, and two lots of $2000 for information that helped. But Grandma Ruby bumped it to $12,000 so we could give the two couples $6000 each. She's not short of a dollar,' Gabi added, seeing a few shocked expressions.

Everyone commented at once, it was a great outcome. I noticed Gabi and Jason exchanging a few curious looks – not that I'm matchmaking, but wouldn't that be good? If only I could match up Mel, sigh.

Jason and I shared something different now; it's hard to explain, but we were closer, tighter, connected. As the Buddhist proverb says, well, I think it's Buddhist – if you saved a life, you were responsible for it – I felt like Jason was watching out for me, a guardian angel. Don't tell Dom.

It was a great happy hour or two hours and great to be home. I would probably need to work over the weekend now to catch up and go through Deidre's spreadsheet so I could hit the ground running with Ed on Monday, but I'm taking my laptop home... I'm not ready yet to be in the office alone after hours.

Tonight, I had Alex's vigil. My work was done, and Gary and Jenny had already paid me. It was now in the hands of the police and their solicitor to prove guilt. It wouldn't be easy – they had motive and Trad placed on location, but how would they prove he pushed Alex? Maybe he'd get off with just an assault charge and live to see another day. He was a ticking time bomb. One day, he would go off.

# Chapter 34

I told Dominic I would be right behind him as the happy hour guests drifted off to start their weekend. Only Jason remained a moment to talk about Alex's case, accepting Gabi and Mel's invitation to meet them at a bar they wanted to try. He promised Dom he would walk me to my car. I think Dom was torn and relieved; I'm sure he would have got on just fine with Jason if I wasn't around.

I sat on the edge of my desk, and Jason lowered himself onto Ed's desk opposite. He crossed his arms and studied me. He looked good, fit, strong, and reliable in his uniform, with his boots and gadgets all adding to the appeal. Who didn't love a man in uniform?

There was a momentary awkward silence, and we rarely do awkward, but then he gave me a quick update on Alex's case.

'I've got some good news.'

I brightened. 'Great. What?'

'Trent's prepared to talk.'

I closed my eyes, exhaled, and silently prayed my thanks. When I opened my eyes, he was smiling at me.

'How did that come about?' I looked at him with even more admiration for closing this case and getting justice for Alex.

Jason shrugged. 'Trad's not a bad guy, and I think becoming a teacher made him reflect on his part in the bullying scenario. He said that he loved connecting with you and some others at the reunion, but he'd never really thought of you all as people before, as likely friends. He was a follower.'

'True,' I agreed. 'Good on him, that takes some courage. Will it be enough to put Trad away?'

'Maybe. The testimony I have says Trad became increasingly enraged that this guy from school, whom he thought was nothing, might have it all, including his girlfriend.'

'That's such a relief,' I said.

Everything was changing, or maybe it was just part of the trauma I was working through. I felt something for Jason; I always did, but after he saved me, it was deeper. It was hard to explain, but I desperately wanted him to hold me and make me feel better. But I knew where that would lead. It wouldn't end well for any of us.

There was tension between us now that wasn't there before or wasn't two-way before −sexual tension.

'How are you?' he asked.

I bit my lower lip for a moment, not liking to put emotions out there and being cautious of getting too intimate with him. I gave a small shrug.

'As you'd expect,' I said. 'I'm fine, really, just going through the stuff that most people do when they've been assaulted.'

'Bit jumpy, not sleeping well, not trusting anyone?' he started.

I nodded and then gave a small laugh, like it was silly. Jason gave me a sympathetic smile.

His voice was tender as he said my name. 'Jesse, there are groups that help with that. I can help with that. Trust me, you are not alone.'

I nodded. I didn't want to get emotional, but I would if he kept talking to me so gently.

'I'm okay, really, I am,' I said, brushing him off.

He continued, ignoring my words. 'You can feel safe in these groups, build yourself up again, and get stronger. The best part is that you can share how you feel with people who get it.' He reached into his pocket, pulled out a piece of paper and, rising, came towards me.

'I've jotted down the best ones, the ones we use all the time,' he said, standing close and offering the list to me. I'm sure his cologne was Armani – strong and sexy.

I took the slip of paper. 'Thank you.'

Jason didn't move back.

'Have you been to any of these?' I asked and looked up at him. Then I realised that might be too personal. 'You don't have to tell me,' I said hurriedly.

He kept looking at me, holding my gaze and was not ashamed to admit he had.

'It's compulsory that we go to several counselling sessions if we're involved in something traumatic. I've been a few times,' he said, putting his hands in his pockets.

'Did it help?' I asked.

He grimaced. 'I'm a guy.'

I laughed. 'Yeah, that you are.'

We looked at each other briefly, and the air was charged. I understood then how affairs started. Someone awakened feelings you haven't felt for some time or made you feel special. I was weak. If the lights were off, you would see the electricity between us. I dropped my gaze from his. I was breathing faster, and if I looked at him, I'd kiss him. There was too much at stake, too much to lose.

*Don't go there. Don't do it.*

I wanted to. The pull to Jason was so intense and immediate. But he did the noble thing.

Clearing his throat, he asked: 'Can I walk you to your car?'

I nodded. 'Yes, please.'

I rose, putting some distance between us, and went around my desk to my laptop. I logged off, grabbed it and my bag and was ready to leave. Jason was locking the windows – he was good at security.

We took the lift to the carpark, conscious of our bond and being within arm's reach of each other. We didn't cross the line that I desperately and wrongly wanted to cross. And the lift didn't break down this time. That was a good thing.

# Chapter 35

THE NEXT NIGHT, SATURDAY, Dominic reached for my hand and held it as we walked Atlas in the cool evening. I broached a topic – something I had to ask him.

'You know when I was in the hospital bed, you said you couldn't do this anymore, wouldn't do it,' I studied him. 'I'm just wondering where your head is at now.'

He sighed and looked away and then back at me.

'I don't like it, Jess. I'm never going to like it. But I've cooled down a bit, and I'm keen on the idea of you hiring security and billing it to the client. But I have a feeling you won't use the service.'

'Depends who provides it,' I said, and he smiled.

'I'm thinking about that too.'

'I don't know how long I will keep doing this, Dom, but I want to do it. I'm going to do it,' I said. I was upfront and surprised myself, but there it was, out there.

His jaw locked, and he said nothing.

We arrived home, and I made a mug of tea for both of us. I carried the mugs out to the front steps where the three of us sat to enjoy the quiet of the night.

'That was a good bonus Gabi gave you. I'm glad she did; you earned it.'

'We earned it,' I said. 'It was generous.'

'You got her a hell of a lot of publicity.'

I agreed. 'Gabi said she had used a publicity company before to boost her profile, paid the same amount as my P.I. fee, and got very little for it. So, I guess she got a very large campaign paid for indirectly by Grandma Ruby's investigation fee. Everyone's happy.'

We sipped our tea, and then I asked: 'So, any ideas on how to spend a $5000 gift voucher from her agency? Mind you, I've got to share half with Ed... he's bound to want a big birthday event. Maybe he'll get hitched!' I shrugged. 'We've got three years before it expires.'

'Got an event in mind?' Dom asked, with a side glance my way.

I smiled. 'Maybe... have you?' I asked.

His hand went to the back of my neck, and he rubbed my shoulders. The bruising around my throat was all but gone, but I was still sore if the right spot was tested.

'I might have,' he said and sipped his tea. 'That would make for one hell of an engagement party.'

'Yeah, if we were a couple that agreed we could stand each other's careers and not want to walk away, it probably would.'

He gave me a smile that didn't reach his eyes and spoke of frustration.

'Think about it, Dom,' I said, putting it back on him. 'You can't still be thinking you want to marry me, given you nearly called it off at my hospital bed.'

He exhaled and put down his tea mug, turning to face me.

'Jess, for better or for worse. I want you to be my wife for life, and if you persist in doing this work, then it's best I'm beside you to protect you any way I can.' He shrugged. 'Yeah, I'm an idiot who loves you blind.'

I laughed and took his hand from my shoulder and kissed it.

'I love you, too. We've got some time before the voucher expires...'

'I'm not waiting three years,' he warned me.

'No, who would?' I agreed, and he grinned at me.

'One day, we could have our own reunion,' Dom said. 'All our kids and grandkids helping to celebrate our wedding anniversary. Jesse Clarke, Jesse Bennato, Jesse Clarke-Bennato?' he said, trying his surname on me. 'It has a ring.'

'I'd be wanting one,' I agreed, teasing him, and then I kissed him, hoping, for now, that might distract him from wedding talk.

It did. It was time to go inside, apparently.


248

THE END.

From the author

**REAL-LIFE RESEARCH:**

Being a journalist and author, I had great fun researching and writing this cosy mystery, just as it was for *Death by Sugar* and *Death by Disguise*.

Should you wish to explore more, I have used elements of truth in all the books – the science experiment in *Death by Sugar*; the techniques of mask making and the very sad story of the Mexican bride in *Death by Disguise*; and the Titanic Mourning Bears and Australian victims in *Death by Reunion*.

Thank you for reading Jesse's third mystery. I hope you enjoyed your time in these pages, and I look forward to crossing paths with you next time Jesse and Dominic venture out. Perhaps you might like to check out some of my other thriller mystery books that follow.

**My sincere thanks to:**

- Art by Karri for designing my covers for the series:

- And Atlas B. Goltz, who lives on in Jesse's tales and my heart forever.

**DEATH BY SUGAR:**

'If you are a fan of Kathryn Ledson or Janet Evanovich (though Jesse Clarke is a lot more reliable, sensible and doesn't over share her personal life as does Stephanie Plumb) you will love unravelling the mysteries in the Jesse Clarke series.' Carol, Reading, Writing and Riesling.

Jesse thought sugar was such a friendly substance until it appeared in two of her cases for all the wrong reasons. Traces of sugar were connected to a bomb that blew up her client's Mercedes. Was the bomb meant to kill, or was it just a warning of what was to come? And could sugar have duped the immune system of a client's mother over thirty years ago, resulting in death?

Juggling the two cases—one in the present and one in the past—Jesse finds herself talking to the living and the dead to get results.

**DEATH BY DISGUISE:**

*'AMAZING! Reading about a female P.I. kicking some ass was just the icing on the cake I needed!'* Christine – Goodreads

The dead are walking and it is not even Halloween!

Sassy private investigator Jesse Clarke knew it wasn't going to be a normal week when two dead people are spotted alive, but their death certificates say otherwise, Spiderman steals a collection of costumes made for the next Comic Con, and Batman drops in to warn her that all is not as it seems.

Supported by her own man of steel—the tall, dark and handsome Dominic; business partner Ed; police contact Officer Jason, who has more than a professional interest in Jesse; and best friend Melanie, Jesse finds herself talking to witches, superheroes and morticians to solve her two cases and looking behind the disguises for answers!

# Also by Helen Goltz

**MISS HAYWARD & THE Detective Series (historical mystery/romance):**
Murder at the Carnival
The Artist's Missing Muse
Mystery at the Asylum
The Mortician's Clue
Murder in Bridal Lane

**The Lady Mortician's Visions (historical mystery/romance/paranormal twist)**
The Missing Brides
The Fake Child
The Dastardly Debutante
The Deathly Dolls
The Potent Perfume
The Watery Grave
More to come....

**The Clairvoyant's Glasses (supernatural/urban fantasy romance)**

Volume 1 – A vision unexpected

Volume 2 – Time has a shadow

Volume 3 – Love knows no bounds

Volume 4 – Fate comes to call

The Raven – Volume 1, coming in 2025


**The Mitchell Parker series published by Next Chapter (crime thrillers):**

Mastermind

Graveyard of the Atlantic

The Fourth Reich


**Writing as Jack Adams (psychological mystery/suspense):**

Poster Girl (stand alone)

Delaney and Murphy childhood friends series:

Asylum

Stalker

Cult

Hitched

Carnival

Forgotten (coming in 2025)

**The Jesse Clarke series (contemporary mysteries):**

Death by Sugar

Death by Disguise

Death by Reunion


**Writing with journalist Chris Adams, The Grave Tales series (non-fiction) x 9 titles:**

Grave Tales: Brisbane Vol.1

Grave Tales: Great Ocean Road – Geelong to Port Fairy

Grave Tales: Sydney Vol.1

Grave Tales: Bruce Highway

Grave Tales: True Crime Vol.1

Grave Tales: Queensland's Great South West

Grave Tales: Melbourne Vol.1

Grave Tales: Queensland's Scenic Rim & Surrounds

Grave Tales: Tasmania.

Grave Tales: Cold Cases (an amalgamation of stories from existing titles)


**Writing as Ally Adams:**

The Saints team (contemporary romance):

Team Lucas

Team Tomas

Team Niklas

Team Alex

**Stand-alone titles:**

The House on Findlater Lane (mystery/romance paranormal)

The Forgotten House (historical romance)

Three Parts Truth (mystery suspense)

Morphers (middle grade fiction).

# About the author

HELEN IS A HYBRID-PUBLISHED, Amazon best-selling author. After studying English Literature, Media, and Communications at universities in Queensland, Australia, and obtaining a Counselling Diploma, Helen has worked as a journalist, producer and marketer in print, TV, radio and public relations. Born in Toowoomba, she has made her home in Logan Village, Australia, with her journalist husband, Chris, and Boxer dog, Baxter. She is published by Next Chapter and her own imprint, Atlas Productions.

Connect with Helen:

Website: www.helengoltz.com

BookBub: www.bookbub.com/authors/helen-goltz

Facebook: www.facebook.com/HelenGoltz.Author

Instagram: https://www.instagram.com/helengoltz1/

# References

**THE TITANIC MOURNING BEAR:**

DeNike, Max, Collectibles, 20 of the Most Valuable Teddy Bears in the World. *Family Minded.* 7 April 2021. Retrieved from URL:

**Titanic Australian survivors:**

Young, Emma, Titanic disaster: the Australian story. *Australian Geographic,* 10 April 2012. Retrieved from URL: